APPREHEND ME NO FLOWERS

Diane Vallere

POLYESTER PRESS BOOKS

"If you are looking for an unconventional mystery with a snarky, no-nonsense main character, this is it…Instead of clashing, humor and danger meld perfectly, and there's a cliffhanger that will make your jaw drop."

— Abigail Ortlieb,
RT Book Reviews

"A charming modern tribute to Doris Day movies and the retro era of the '50s, including murders, escalating danger, romance…and a puppy!"

— Linda O. Johnston,
Author of the Pet Rescue Mysteries

"I love mysteries where I can't figure out who the real killer is until the end, and this was one of those. The novel was well written, moved at a smooth pace, and Madison's character was a riot."

— *ChickLit Plus*

APPREHEND ME NO FLOWERS

A Mad for Mod Mystery

A Polyester Press Mystery

Polyester Press

www.polyesterpress.com

This is a work of fiction. Characters, places, and events are the product of the author's imagination or are used fictitiously. Any resemblance to real people, companies, institutions, organizations, or incidents is entirely coincidental. No affiliation with Doris Day or Universal is claimed or implied.

Cover design by Diane Vallere. Rocky (dog) Artwork © Henery Press, used with permission

eBook ISBN: 9781939197863

Paperback ISBN: 9781939197870

Hardcover ISBN: 9781939197887

❀ Created with Vellum

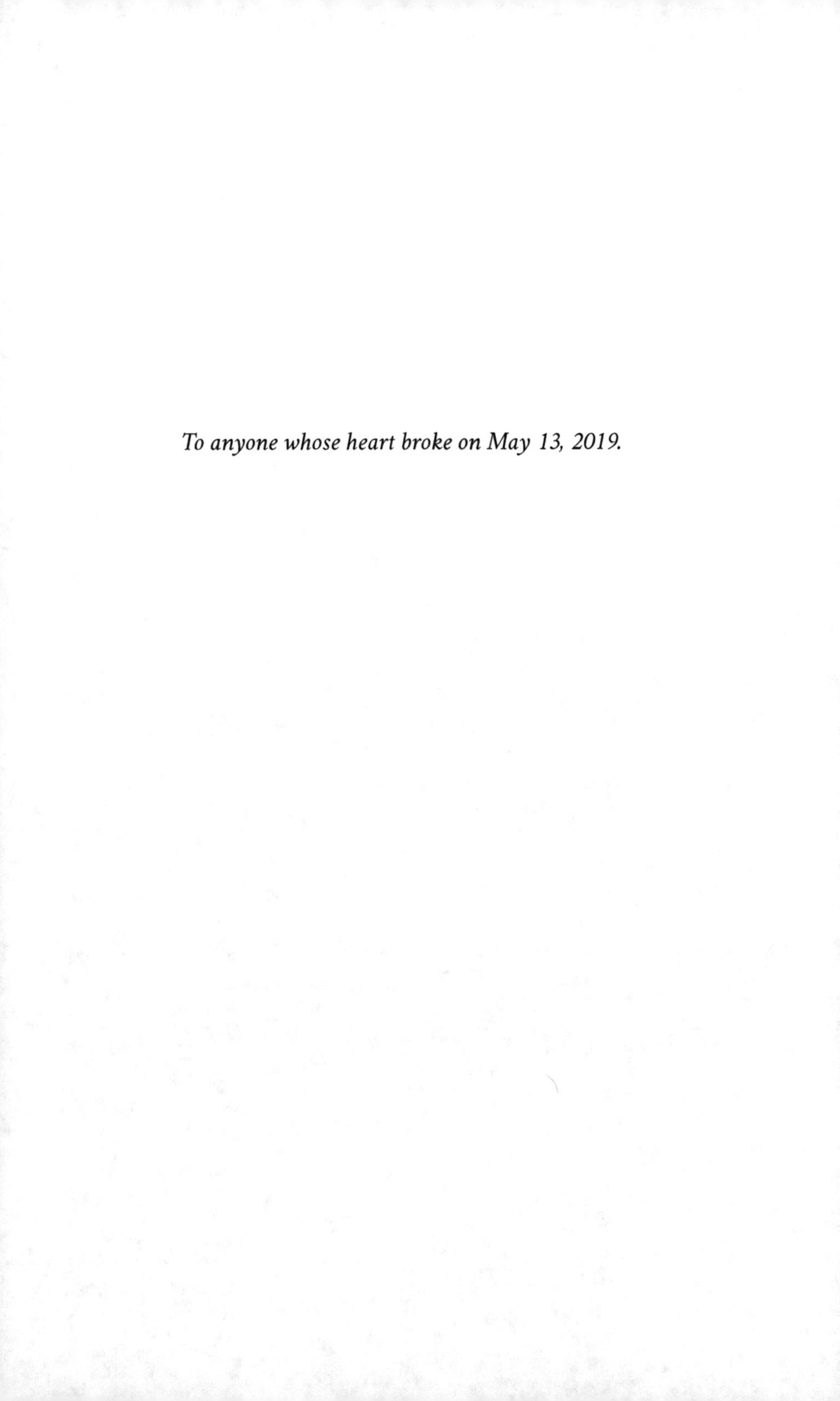

To anyone whose heart broke on May 13, 2019.

ACKNOWLEDGMENTS

Thank you to: the Madison Night fans who patiently waited for a new book. Also to: Henery Press, and to Mary Moon, Craig Marquis, and Carol Kelly for offering to be dead people who left behind super snazzy wardrobes for Madison.

Tʜᴇ ꜰʟᴏᴡᴇʀs ᴡᴇʀᴇ ᴀ ɴɪᴄᴇ ᴛᴏᴜᴄʜ.

"Sorry I'm late," Tex said, handing me a bouquet of daisies. The grocery-store price tag was still affixed to the green butcher paper wrapped around their stems. "Garcia got called to his kids' school and left me with a staffing problem." He leaned over and kissed me. It seemed a risky move considering we'd been keeping our relationship quiet, but the woods surrounding the White Rock Lake picnic area were relatively private. Rocky, my caramel-and-white Shih Tzu, and his best friend, Wojo, a Shi Chi puppy, hopped around Tex's feet, happy to have something new to sniff.

White Rock Lake was about four miles from Thelma Johnson's house. Thelma Johnson's house was technically my house, after paying the back taxes on the property a few years ago, but the circumstances surrounding the purchase made it awkward to call it mine.

"I haven't been here that long myself," I said.

"I thought we said six-thirty?"

"We did." I poured spring water into a blue plastic tumbler and transferred the flowers from their wax paper to the makeshift vase.

Tex lowered himself onto the bench across from me. "You're lying, aren't you?"

"I'm lying."

I handed him a sandwich marked with a piece of blue painter's tape. We had similar taste in lunchmeat, but Tex had an affinity for vinegar that I lacked. He tore open a bag of potato chips while I uncovered a container of coleslaw and handed him a fork.

There was no point pretending I'd shown up minutes before Tex. His job, captain of the Lakewood Police Department, kept him busy, and short staffing made it worse. My job, owner of a mid-century modern decorating business, allowed me to work whenever I wanted, though a lawsuit forced me to shutter my doors indefinitely. Between our two extenuating circumstances, Tex's were better. Hands down.

"Don't worry about me," I said. "I spent the day organizing the attic. Last year, I moved all the clothing and wardrobe items from my storage locker to my house, but I never took the time to sort through my recent acquisitions." I stood, held my hands out to the sides, and spun slowly to show off a red-and-blue floral overblouse dress. It buttoned up the back and had a decorative bow on the front. Fat pleats hung down from a drop waist, the hem hitting above my shiny red rain boots.

"Maybe some day you'll buy out the estate of a former pinup girl. They're your era too, right?"

I sat down and held a container of salad while Tex portioned a serving onto his plate.

"Night, you know this is temporary, right?"

"Which part? Me having too much time on my hands, or you not having enough?" I gave Tex a pause in which to answer, though my question was largely rhetorical. It, like most of the difficulties with our relationship, was something to manage around. "It is what it is."

Tex and I had planned to meet for a late picnic after his daily responsibilities had ended. The temperature was in the mid-eighties, and dark clouds overhead threatened rain at any moment. The combination kept most people in enclosed, air-conditioned environments, which made this the perfect setting for a private outing.

"I meant us," he said, gesturing back and forth between us. "This."

"We're temporary? Thank you for clearing that up. Nothing like going into a relationship with the expectation that the end is in sight."

"You know that's not what I meant. It's not an easy time to be a cop, and I don't want any anti-police sentiment to rub off on you."

"We've been through this before. I told you, I understand. The lawsuit isn't exactly making me look good either. I'd prefer to keep you from that."

We lapsed into silence while we took turns passing Tupperware of food back and forth. It was possible we were thinking the same thing: if our relationship were destined to crash and burn, it was better that we'd be the only two to deal with the fallout. It wasn't my most optimistic thought, but it was about a fifty percent probability.

"How's Garcia doing on desk duty?"

"He appears to be taking it in stride. It's a shame things went down for him as they did, but rules are rules."

Officer Garcia was a rookie cop who was responsible for the most recent blight on the Lakewood Police Department's public record. Having fulfilled six months of desk duty, he'd been sent on patrol with a tenured officer who had trouble holding onto a partner. On Garcia's first night in the field, while managing a domestic dispute, his gun discharged, accidentally shooting the resident's coffee table. Turns out nothing resolves a marital spat quite like a united front against the police. Charges were pressed, an investigation ensued, and Garcia was back behind the front desk where the most damage he could do was burn the coffee.

Local politics had put police departments under scrutiny, and Tex, who was better at finding answers than covering up problems, was soon called out for rising crime rates and low police retention. Budgetary decisions from the city reallocated money from Lakewood to Highland Park, the nearby affluent neighborhood where the property owners and high estate values demanded protection.

As higher-paying positions opened in the neighboring police departments, Tex had no choice but to support the transfer requests of his officers who'd been capped at part-time work in his precinct. Open jobs led to budgetary excess, which led to budget cuts, which led to Tex working sixty-hour weeks.

When Tex and I started dating, we both tried not to talk about work. For two people whose lives had been defined by our careers, a sudden interest in network TV seemed a poor excuse for common ground. At first, it was uncomfortable sharing my deepest fears about profit margin and now the lawsuit, but Tex proved to be a nonjudgmental listener. Fortunately for him, he already knew I was comfortable talking about his daily life.

"What about your meeting?" I asked.

"I got stood up."

Tex and I were at opposite ends of the problems-with-work situation. The lawsuit temporarily shut down Mad for Mod and left me with too much time on my hands. Tex, on the other hand, was stretched thin. We'd spent last month brainstorming fundraisers for his precinct, and while the idea of a chili cookoff sounded amusing, it would barely put a dent in the needs of the local police force. Tex figured go big or go home and reached out to local businessmen with deep pockets. He'd scored a meeting with Winston Burr, a bigshot in Dallas who had a reputation for giving back to the community.

"How about you?" Tex asked. "Any progress?"

"After the attic temperature became unbearable, I defrosted the freezer."

"Nothing new on the lawsuit?"

"Nothing new on the lawsuit. Nothing new anywhere. I'm not used to having free time, and it's starting to get to me. Tomorrow I might get the service manual out of my glovebox and learn how to do an oil change on my Alfa Romeo."

Tex squinted at my pleated floral dress. "You need to borrow a T-shirt and jeans?"

"I found a box of vintage coveralls in the attic. One of the estates I bought out belonged to an airplane parts factory worker."

Tex held his hands up. "Don't look at me like I'm your next project. You can wear dead people's clothes, but I like my polo shirts and Wranglers fine."

"Are you done?" I asked. When he grinned, I continued. "It belonged to a woman. Can you imagine? A woman assembling airplane parts on the factory floor in the early sixties. I bet she didn't let anybody boss her around."

We finished our picnic and packed up the trash. I pulled the daisies out of the makeshift vase and rewrapped the stems in a scrap of plastic wrap. These were fresh and would remain in bloom for a few days if nurtured.

"How about we go for a walk?" Tex asked.

"Sure. Can you put the picnic basket and the flowers in the Jeep? I'll toss the trash."

I looped the two dog leashes over my wrist and carried the trash to the closest bin. An unpleasant, pungent smell hit me as I approached. The next closest trash can was across the park, and even from a distance, I could tell it was overflowing. I pulled the neckline of my dress up over my nose and mouth and pulled off the lid.

Inside the bin was a black plastic garbage bag. The top had been knotted, but the plastic had split open. I leaned closer and quickly looked away. Inside the plastic was the one thing I'd hoped to never see again.

A dead body.

2

THIS WASN'T MY FIRST TIME FINDING SOMETHING UNUSUAL IN THE trash, though the smell and the presence of maggots made the discovery among the least pleasant. I turned away and gagged even though Dacron polyester was still covering my mouth. I knew better than to leave Tex and my picnic trash in the bin. I stumbled away toward the car.

"Tex?" I called. My voice came out muffled. Yelling louder required a deeper breath.

To my distant right, a twig snapped. I rushed the dogs back to the parking lot. As soon as I saw Tex by the car, my arms went limp, and our picnic trash fell to the ground.

I yanked the fabric away from my face and pointed over my shoulder. "There's a body in a trash can," I said. "About two hundred feet straight ahead. I can show you if you—"

"Did you touch it?"

"I used a stick to hold the bag open. There are maggots." I led him back to the trash can and held the stick out toward him. It exchanged hands, and he did what I did and reacted how I reacted.

"Go wait in the Jeep," he said. He handed me his keys.

I knew Tex's command had to do with my safety, but the body I'd seen had been dead for more than a few hours. I'd recently watched a documentary about forensic entomology and knew the presence of bugs would help a medical examiner determine the time of death and possibly a few other things the naked eye couldn't discern. Plus, Tex and I had spent the past forty-five minutes leisurely dining on sandwiches, chips, and coleslaw. If a murderer had been here, he or she would have likely fled when we arrived.

"It's dark, and it's raining. Any clues are going to be obliterated by weather and critters overnight. I don't know what else we're going to find out here, but I know you need my help."

"Right now, I need the dogs out of the way."

Rocky and Wojo strained their leashes, and their barks comingled. I placed our trash bag in the back of the Jeep and opened the car door. The three of us climbed inside. The prediction of rain had led Tex to put the top on, which made the issue of canine containment easier. Muddy paws left marks on the skirt of my dress, though through the wonders of polyester, the fabric would easily clean. Seconds later, after it became obvious they wanted back out, I opened the door and held their leashes while they sniffed the parking lot.

Tex returned a few minutes later. "I thought I told you to wait in the car," he said.

"The dogs were going wild, and I thought we would have heard if someone else was here. Besides, I saw bugs on the body. Maggots?" I asked. Tex nodded. "That means the body has been there for a few days."

"All true, but that doesn't mean you should take unnecessary risks." He scooped up Wojo and held the small puppy by his chest. Like my dress, Tex's T-shirt was soon covered in muddy footprints. Wojo raised his nose and pushed it into the gap between Tex's arm and his body.

Something about Tex calmly holding his dog in the parking lot felt off. "Did you call it in?" I asked.

Tex didn't answer right away. Rocky, wanting to be held too, stood on his hind legs and put his paws on my knees. He whined and repositioned his back paws, keeping his balance while vying for attention. I held his leash securely but kept my eyes on Tex.

"It's after hours. Technically, I'm the first officer on the scene. I'd like to get a record of things before calling in the cavalry. The rain is going to destroy any evidence left behind, and I could use a second set of eyes."

I nodded. I took Wojo from him and opened the door to the Jeep.

"Bring the dogs," Tex said.

A Shih Tzu and a Shi Chi weren't exactly bloodhounds, but I supposed they were better than nothing.

We returned to the picnic site. "Do you know what you're looking for?" I asked.

"Anything that doesn't fit."

It wasn't a snarky comment. I'd once made the case that my decorator's eye qualified me to assess a crime scene as effectively as his detective skills did him. He hadn't liked the comparison, but he'd come to learn it was at least partially true. Allowing me to insert myself into his crime scene walk-through had less to do with our relationship than the possibility that I'd see something he'd missed.

We advanced slowly, taking in every detail. When Tex turned

to the left, I turned to the left. When he turned to the right, I turned to the right. When the phone he held rang, I pulled out mine, expecting it to ring too. It did not.

"Allen," Tex answered. After a short pause, he said, "Where are they?" He turned his back on me and walked a few feet away.

Rocky pulled me toward a hedge that ran the perimeter of the park. Tex's voice faded in the background. A break in the hedge revealed a clear view of neatly manicured cemetery grounds on the other side. I peered through the hedges. A circular drive cut through the grass, leading past a sizeable mausoleum at the far right and a mortuary at the left. Evenly spaced marble tombstones peppered the lawn between them.

"Yo, Night," Tex said, startling me by his unexpected proximity. "You better take the dogs back to the car and get comfortable."

"Why? What's wrong?" I asked when I saw the look on his face.

"I'm going to be here for a while."

"That was the cavalry?"

"Not exactly. That was one of my officers. He took a call from a couple of hikers who found a body in a trash can on the opposite side of the park."

"*Another* body?" I asked.

Tex nodded. A flash of lightning lit up his face, enhancing dark circles and frown lines that had been carved in over time thanks to the stresses of his job. "The hikers claim they opened the bag, saw what was inside, and stepped away. They left their phones in the car, so they had to hike back to where they parked before calling it in."

"Where was that?" I asked, looking across the lake. The oppressive humidity and weather conditions had left me sure we'd been alone. It hadn't occurred to me that we had company.

"A nursery about half a mile down Garland Road."

"Do you believe them?"

"Sounds like they fit the part: granolas who want to save the world but got scared by nature taking its course."

I held up my hands. "Let's not judge too harshly, okay? I think anybody who finds a body in a public trash receptacle is going to have a less than honorable reaction."

The air was thick with rain. Lights were placed intermittently around the gravel drive that ran around the circumference of the lake, casting odd shadows in the dark.

"What does it mean?" I asked.

"It means we'll need to find another picnic spot," he said. "The closest patrol car was five minutes away," he continued. "By the time they arrived, the hikers had moved their car to the street, but they were waiting inside. The engine was running, and Clark said the heater was on."

"It's eighty-five degrees."

"Fits with the reaction one might have after discovering a body in a trash can. You go into a form of shock. Disbelief that you saw what you think you saw. If their story is accurate, then adrenaline carried them to their car, through the phone call, and out of the park. After they sat for a minute with no tasks to accomplish, the adrenaline would wear off, and their shock would set in. Classic physical manifestation of shock is getting the chills. What would you do if you got the chills in your car?"

"Turn on the heater."

Tex nodded. "So, without vetting their statement, I'd have to say they seem legit."

"What next?"

"My officer verified the presence of a body. There was enough visual evidence to confirm the body wasn't alive. He radioed the medical examiner and then called it in to me."

As captain, Tex didn't normally go on body-in-a-trash-bin calls. But taking the promotion to captain had been an unexpected move for a whole lot of reasons, and even though Tex made a great captain, he missed the realities of the field.

I listened to Tex but kept my eyes on the ground. Something blue caught my attention. I bent over and peered closer at the ground and made out a pile of faded blue petals. "Did you see these?"

"What are they?"

I pointed. "Looks like rose petals. There weren't any roses in the flowers you brought, were there?"

"I brought daisies. Where are they? Where's our trash?"

"In the back seat of the car. I didn't think you'd want me to leave it here."

Tex pulled a plastic bag out of his pocket. He flipped the bag inside out, picked up a pinch of the petals, and flipped the bag to the right side out. He sealed the bag and handed it to me.

"What am I supposed to do with it?" I asked.

"Put it in the car," he said. "Better yet, get a bag out of the back and bring it here."

I trudged back to the car and found a Whole Foods bag behind Tex's seat. When I locked up the car and started back, I noticed he had wandered to the right. I put the evidence bag inside the tote, slung it over my shoulder, and took the rudimentary footpath to the left side of the tree line.

The distance I put between me and Tex had less to do with canvassing the area than the stability of the path. I'd suffered a torn ACL years ago, reinjured it more than once, and now walked with a limp. The cliché of feeling weather in my joint had turned out to be true, and I wasn't going to risk a reinjury with a hike in the dark across slippery grass.

As I neared the tree line, the light from Tex's flashlight dimmed, and I had to rely on my phone. Feet scuttled through the brush, and I told myself it was one of the dogs and not the more likely rodent or snake.

I tightened my grip on the two leashes with my left hand. I'd known dating Tex would get complicated, but I didn't know it would get this complicated this fast. "I'll talk to you later," I said. I hesitated, unsure if there would be a kiss goodnight or not.

Tex leaned forward and brushed his lips against mine. When he pulled away, he said, "I'm sorry, Night. I can't let you leave."

Sirens sounded in the distance. Experience told me the quiet of the lake was about to be blown apart by cops and news vans, and there was little I wanted less than to be connected to another homicide.

3

THERE WAS NO SENSE ARGUING. ANY VEHICLE SEEN LEAVING THE site where two bodies had been discovered would be stopped, and my being behind the wheel of Tex's Jeep at said site would shift attention from the case to what we were hiding. We'd always known things would unfold in due course; due course came on a rainy Thursday in late May.

The downpour came suddenly. I waited in the Jeep and watched through a film of rain as two cop cars, an ambulance, and a gray sedan parked in the spaces around me. The team worked in tandem to move the body, illuminate the woods, and canvas the area to make sure they hadn't missed anything. Tex pointed to the bag and the trees. He indicated the ground and then gestured in wide, sweeping circles as if telling his team to spread out and leave nothing behind. At the rate the weather was interfering, whatever evidence was there would be gone before morning.

Tex was right about the temperature. I had the heater running at full blast and couldn't get warm. I'd turned fifty-one three months ago; where's a hot flash when you need it?

Hours later, Tex returned to the Jeep. The insistent sound of rain pelting the canvas top of the Jeep had put me to sleep, and I woke with a crick in my neck. Tex opened the door, lifted me, and carried me to the passenger side. I was only marginally awake and protested, but he ignored me. He buckled me in and returned to the driver's side, and I fell back asleep before we pulled onto the main road.

It's unclear how I made it into the house or up the stairs to the bedroom. When I woke, the first thing I noticed was my peignoir set lying on a chair in the bedroom where I'd left them the previous morning. I peeked under the covers. I was wearing a Lakewood Police Department T-shirt and floral cotton panties.

On top of the thin sheet were the two dogs. My gradual stirring woke them both, and soon I was covered in sloppy canine kisses. I threw back the sheet and got up then pulled on a yellow bathing suit and a bubblegum-pink wraparound dress over top. It was five forty-five, and the sun was cresting, spreading a warm glow above the horizon. I slipped into a pair of navy-blue Keds and went downstairs. Tex was at my kitchen table. He drank coffee from a gray Lakewood Police Department mug that he left behind for times when yellow-and-white daisy mugs threatened his masculinity.

"I didn't hear you get up," I said.

"I couldn't sleep." His eyes were red. He turned his head and coughed into his elbow.

"You've been up all night?"

He nodded. "After half an hour of staring at the ceiling, I came down here. No point keeping you awake too."

Of the two of us, I was the morning person. I regularly woke in the five a.m. range and headed to Crestwood Pool to swim laps. Once a week, I convinced Tex to join me, but his hours quickly dictated that I let him sleep when he wanted. We'd known each other for four years, and it surprised me that until recently, I had no idea what his day-to-day life was like.

I filled a vintage yellow mug with coffee and stared out the window at the property next to me. A For Sale sign jutted out of the lawn in front of a small square building. "Did you take anything?" I asked while I watched a bird land on the sign. "Melatonin or Tylenol PM?"

"I don't take medication," he said. "I need a clear head." He held up his coffee cup.

"Caffeine's temporary. As much as you like to think you're Superman, you're not."

"This is my job."

"Come on, Tex. I know what you do for a living, and I know how committed you are to doing it. You need a break, or you're going to get sick." I took a sip and closed my eyes. The dogs joined us and buried both of their heads in Rocky's bowl, leaving Wojo's food untouched.

"Dead bodies aren't conveniently scheduled around circadian rhythms and migraines."

I joined him at the table. "Tell me what kept you awake."

"You know I can't talk about my cases," he said.

"Do you have a case? You have two bodies. I already know that. I saw one firsthand. Before I dozed off in the car, the scene was hopping. If the press was there, the rest of Dallas is going to know everything I know when the morning news airs. Surely you can preempt them by a couple of hours."

Tex raised his mug and drank then set it on top of a yellow, green, and white knitted coaster. There had been a time when Tex in my house felt incongruous, but—heck, why lie? Tex may have accepted my quirky yellow-and-white kitchen, but he'd always look out of place.

"You can't keep me out of this one," I said.

Rocky cowered for a moment like I'd caught him doing something wrong.

I calmed my voice and continued. "It's a matter of time before someone knocks on my door to get a statement. You know how much the press love me these days."

Decades ago, I'd honed my decorator's eye by watching Doris Day movies, studying the sets, and internalizing the elements that were true to the era.

But on May thirteenth, the news of screen legend Doris Day's death reached me from every angle. The phone exploded. I'd become known as a local authority on Doris Day prior to her passing thanks to volunteer work at the local retro cinema theater and a resemblance to her screen presence. After turning down half a dozen interviews, I saw the opportunity to introduce a new audience to her legacy. After the lawsuit became public, the articles became less than flattering. The result was a level of notoriety that the six murder investigations I'd been involved with had not.

My life has been, shall we say, unique.

"The press is still harassing you?"

"Reporters have been knocking on my door since the lawsuit became public. When they find you in my kitchen, they're going to draw conclusions. If you don't want this"—I gestured between us—"to interfere with your job on the force, then letting it be known that I found one of the bodies gives you a convenient excuse for being here."

"You know, Night, not that I don't admire how you think, but I can't tell if you're helping me or using me."

"Using you for what?"

"Distraction."

I took another sip of coffee. "Would that be so bad?"

He leaned back and ran his hands over his dark-blond hair. The circles under his eyes were more pronounced in the daylight. He was dressed in a black polo shirt and faded Wranglers, his off-duty uniform of choice. If he planned to go into the station, he was either taking extreme liberties with the dress code, or he kept a change of clothes in his office.

He took another pull on his coffee and then set the mug down and stood. "You want to know what I know? Sit. Listen. But this goes no further than this kitchen. Got it?"

"Sure."

I dropped into a chair, and Tex paced back and forth. "Last night, two hikers discovered a body in the trash can by the entrance to White Rock Lake. The body was naked and appeared to have been thoroughly cleaned."

"Like the body we found."

"Right. It started raining about the time they called the police. A patrol cop took the call from dispatch and called me. Two more heard about it on the scanner and called a lightning team. The medical examiner showed up next."

"The graduation party."

"More like a scavenger hunt. With two bodies on opposite sides of the park, it's hard to say which location, if either, was the crime scene."

"Or if the victims were killed elsewhere and the bodies moved after the crime."

"How did you come up with that theory?"

"The bodies were naked and appeared to have been washed.

That seems to indicate someone wanted to remove evidence and cover their tracks."

"Agreed." He stared at me for a moment and then resumed pacing. "After I put you to bed, I went back out. We expanded the preliminary search from the immediate area to the whole park and turned up some discarded fast food packages, two used condoms, and a couple of dirty magazines. Maybe we'll get a DNA match or a lead. Everything was bagged and tagged and taken to the station."

"Do you have any information on the victims?"

"Not yet. Lloyd – the medical examiner – got to the scene after one. He took possession and moved the bodies to the morgue for an autopsy. There's significant damage to both, and he's not confident we'll be able to release photos to the public."

"It's that bad?"

Tex stared at his coffee for a few seconds before he spoke again. "We don't know anything about the victim. Victims. Either one of them."

"No wallets? No identification? Nothing else in the trash?"

"Nothing."

"Then what now?"

"Ideally, Lloyd will find something we can use."

"You haven't mentioned Lloyd before. Is he new?"

"Yes. He has a private practice in West Lawn. The city cut the ME staff, so now we hire out. Lloyd's still a little green." Tex gave me the closest thing to a smile he'd mustered all morning.

"Give him time to get acclimated to the job," I added. "He's probably figuring out how to connect with you."

Tex's phone rang, and he answered before the first ring finished. "You got something for me?"

I nursed my coffee while Tex scribbled notes on the back of an unopened piece of junk mail. He asked a few questions but mostly said yes and no, two are you sure's, and a thank you. Before the call ended, he requested photos be emailed to him. He disconnected and leaned back.

"A man and a woman. Man in his sixties. Woman in her thirties. Time of death over a week ago."

"Any identifying characteristics?"

"None. I've got two unidentified bodies that nobody seems to be missing." He crossed his arms and stared at me for a few seconds. I could tell he was deep in thought.

"What are you going to do now?" I finally asked.

"Knock on doors and ask around the neighborhood. Somebody might have seen something." Neither one of us said it, but I knew it wasn't a lot to go on. "Somebody other than you. For now, I'm keeping you out of it."

4

THE TROUBLE WITH TEX'S CASE WASN'T THAT HE HAD A HOMICIDE on his hands. Sure, that was bad enough, and double the victims made it double the work. But he was jumping off an unfortunate distance from the starting line. Almost a day after the discovery of the bodies, and he still didn't even know who they were. Why wasn't anybody looking for them?

"You said there were maggots. That helps establish a timeline, right? The gestation period of a maggot should tell you something."

Tex held his hand up to cut me off. "Is it too late to request that my girlfriend not use phrases like 'gestation period of a maggot'?"

"Am I your girlfriend?" I asked, somewhat surprised.

"Outside of this house, you're the annoying woman who keeps showing up in my cases."

After our first date went better than we both expected, Tex and I were faced with a decision. Have a normal relationship like normal people or keep things quiet so we could contain any possible damage when it (almost inevitably) didn't work out. Tex was a womanizing homicide detective, and I was a decorator who dressed like Doris Day. We were anything but normal. The decision was easy.

"What about the missing persons reports?" I asked, shifting the conversation to a less controversial subject.

Tex narrowed his eyes and stared at me. I waited for him to answer. I misunderstood his silence to mean he thought it was a ridiculous suggestion, so I defended it. "You have two unidentified bodies. A man and a woman. If someone reported a couple missing and you can match up the timeline, then you might ID them that way. You said yourself they've been there a couple of days. That means wherever they've been, they probably weren't where they usually are, and if they have friends or family around here, someone may have reported them missing."

Tex spun his computer to face me. On the screen was a missing persons database. "I've been going through this since I got home."

"And?"

"So far, nothing."

"I guess you can't leak images of their bodies to the press," I said, half under my breath.

"Why not?"

"If the bodies were unidentifiable when you found them, I doubt their pictures would be recognizable. The images would scare the public more than anything."

Tex pushed his computer away. "How'd you get like this?"

This discussion had come up before, and every time I'd successfully danced around it. What Tex wanted to know was how a supposedly nice woman like me had gotten desensitized about life. It wasn't something I chose to overanalyze.

"How'd I get like what?" I asked, feigning ignorance. I raised my mug to my lips and sipped.

"Like this. Drinking coffee and talking about maggots and unidentifiable bodies. And don't try to tell me that comes with the territory of being a decorator. I know that much."

I set my mug down. "Come on, Tex, we've been over this a hundred times before. We have the same skillset; we use it in different careers. Used. Past tense."

An awkward silence stretched between us. It was becoming part of our routine. Every time the subject of my career came up, Tex waited for me to say something to let him know where the lawsuit stood. And every time, I dismissed the conversation.

I left Tex to his missing persons database and drove to the pool. I might have caught a few hours of sleep last night, but that didn't mean I didn't have a lot on my mind. For Tex, throwing himself into his case was the way to clear his mental clutter. For me, it was the Zen of swimming laps.

I arrived later than usual thanks to our recap of the previous night and ended up sharing a lane with two seniors who claimed they were leaving soon. I dove into the water and propelled my body forward. I thought about the question Tex had wanted me to answer. The morning swim was my therapy session; the pool was the doctor's office.

Most people wouldn't count being sued among their favorite experiences, and I was no exception. When the papers were first delivered to Mad for Mod, indicating me as the defendant and Brandon Montgomery as the accuser in a case of misrepresentation, stolen designs, and fraud, I admit, my first thought was that it was a joke.

Mad for Mod started out as a one-woman show. I never set out to be the richest person in the decorating line of work, but I provided niche services for loyal customers, and that was good enough for me. Flashier companies offered architectural services and demolition or flat fees for quickie renovations. My business model was different: walk me through your room. Show me your favorite items. Consult with me on a vision board and a proposal. Work alongside me if you want so you can have a satisfying memory of the renovation and we can discuss revisions on the fly.

The people who hired me came via referrals and word-of-mouth. Those who tended toward Design Within Reach as their jumping-off point inevitably hired a design firm instead, and I was fine with that. Mid-century modern wasn't the most popular decorating style, but it was what I loved. I'd rather be surrounded by like minds than fat wallets.

Which might explain why the lawsuit caught me by surprise.

In the legal case of Montgomery vs. Mad for Mod, I was being accused of having stolen the designs of one Brandon Montgomery, the owner of a local design firm. He'd been hired to renovate the showroom of By George, a wedding planner in the West End, but too many missed deadlines had left the client unhappy and the job unfinished.

After four weeks of zero contact from Brandon or anyone at Montgomery HQ, the wedding planner reached out to me to take over the job. I'd said yes with the intention to present my own concept and furnish the site with items from my sizeable inventory.

But before I had a chance to complete a proposal, the news of Doris Day's death reached me. Instead of presenting a fresh design for By George, I completed the one in progress by following Brandon's plans and executing them to the letter. The client was pleased and paid my invoice in full.

By the weekend, my calendar was filled with requests for

interviews and quotes, stories about Doris Day's influence on my decorating style.

Here's where things went wonky. When asked, in a wrap-up question, about my recent commissions, I mentioned the job at By George. I showed photos of my work. I took credit for a design that wasn't mine. Two days later, Brandon Montgomery filed a lawsuit against Mad for Mod.

It wasn't until the phone rang with clients canceling out of jobs that I felt the implications. By the time the op-ed piece "Mad for Malpractice?" was published in the *Dallas Morning News*, outlining the charges against me and asking additional plaintiffs to come forward with statements about my unprofessional practices, I realized how much I had to lose.

Swimming laps had the desired effect of clearing my mind. The monotony of churning through laps hypnotized me, and soon all thoughts of lawsuits, maggots, and bodies were forgotten. I swam to the end of the lane and glided into the wall, relaxed and at peace with the world.

And when I raised my head and saw security consultant Donna Nast standing on the deck with her arms crossed and her scowl on, that inner peace became a distant memory.

5

Donna Nast, aka "Nasty" as she was referred to behind her back at the police department where she used to work, was not easily categorized. She was twenty years younger than me, a former police officer turned business owner of Big Bro Security, a still-expanding start-up that continued its growth trajectory years after being hatched. She was also one of Tex's former girlfriends.

The circumstances surrounding a recent life-and-death situation had made it less difficult to hate her, though she didn't go out of her way to breed warm and fuzzy vibes between us. Despite this, I'd developed a begrudging respect for her, and when a court ordered an injunction against Mad for Mod, I turned to her, not my friends, for advice.

Donna had long, copper-highlighted hair and a figure that was on the slim side of curvaceous. Today she wore a low-cut black men's undershirt, revealing ample cleavage, and snug skinny jeans. Her clothes hugged every one of her curves—including her current six-month pregnant belly.

"I have some good news," she said. "Meet me in the locker room and make it quick. I can think of twenty places I'd rather be than here."

"We have an agreement," I said. "You can't keep threatening to back out." I pulled myself out of the water and tucked my cap and goggles under the side of my bathing suit.

"How many times do I have to tell you we don't have an agreement? My help is informal."

"Then draw up the paperwork and make it formal."

"I can't take your money, Madison."

"And I can't be your charity case."

"That would imply you were a case."

Nasty wasn't one for small talk. She communicated like a man. Brevity and directness, no warm fuzzies. Yet somehow, she was the sexiest woman in any room she inhabited. It was one of life's mysteries. It had gone against every natural impulse that I had to approach Nasty with questions about my lawsuit, but in the end, it was a need for advice that overrode my pettiness.

Nasty followed me into the locker room. "Sorry about my attitude," she said unexpectedly. "It's the hormones. They make me act like a regular woman. I've spent years training against that, and now a tiny millionaire is manipulating me."

Nasty was referring not to the baby within her but the father of the baby, Gerry Rose. He was a seventy-something, highly successful architect, owning a firm that kept an in-house team to design and build out pockets of the greater Dallas area. Despite his short stature, he believed bigger was better and led the movement to bulldoze communities that had been planned in the post-war era and build McMansions for the growing families of Dallas. I didn't like his business model, and when he offered to absorb Mad for Mod into his company, I'd been caught off guard. A brief conversation told me the truth: what he liked were my client loyalty rate and my independence.

It was what I liked too. Despite us agreeing on that, I turned him down.

I removed my bathing suit and showered off the chlorine. It was fitting that, having already seen the most private parts of my business, Nasty would now see the most private parts of me. I wrapped myself in a towel and got my clothes out of my locker. Nasty leaned against a wall, reading something on her phone.

"I'll be ready in a minute," I said, heading to a privacy stall to dress.

"Don't flatter yourself, Madison. You're not my type."

I ignored her comment (mostly) and pulled the curtain on the privacy stall closed anyway.

"I did some digging into Brandon Montgomery's client list," Nasty said. "He's worked with some wealthy families. It's not normal for this level of Dallas society to go with someone who pulled what he pulled, so I'm in the process of getting statements from each of them. I'd be willing to bet he's got connections on his family tree that open a lot of doors."

"I thought you said you had good news?" I asked through the curtain.

"I do. I may have found a loophole that'll allow you to keep your business license."

I pulled a blue-and-white sleeveless top over a blue knit skirt and coordinating blue-and-cream jacket, wrapped my suit, cap, and goggles in my wet towel, and jammed it all into my bag. I slung the bag on my shoulder, hooked my fingers into my Keds, and pulled the curtain open. Nasty was still reading her phone. I doubted she'd looked up once during our conversation.

"I don't want to be a pessimist, but if I lose this lawsuit, I'll lose everything," I said. "Brandon is suing for payment for the job in the West End, for reimbursement of materials he claims I removed from the job and disposed of, and for monetary compensation for his unrealized ideas. These aren't the kinds of things that have a price tag, and he knows it. If he wins, it won't matter if I have my business license. He'll get everything: my inventory and my client list. I'll have nothing left."

Nasty clicked her phone off and dropped it into an expensive handbag. She tipped her head so her long, copper-streaked hair fell over one shoulder, and she stared at me with an expression that suggested I was a jumble of numbers and she was a mathematician. "How'd you start Mad for Mod? When you moved here?"

"I filled out paperwork for a DBA—Doing Business As— applied for a business loan from the bank, established a line of credit, found a vacant storefront—"

She held up her hand to cut me off. "Not the details. The actual business model. How did you make it happen?"

I didn't brag about the early days of Mad for Mod, because what gave me my start was often the same thing that turned off potential clients and friends.

"I studied the obituaries to identify women of a certain age and reached out to their next-of-kin to acquire their estates. I drove around Dallas on trash day and collected things people threw out. I watched YouTube videos and learned how to refinish discarded items. The things that were beyond my abilities went to local handymen and carpenters for restoration."

"Exactly. You did things other people think are unpleasant. You built your company on a penny and a prayer, and what you couldn't do yourself, you hired out. You can do that again. The thing you need to make it is that business license. The obits are still going to give you leads. You'll find another handyman. You can go back to finding junk on street corners if you need to, but if you lose that license, you'll be a middle-aged woman with a can of primer."

"What's the loophole?" I asked.

She stared at me.

"The loophole. That you found. That's going to let me keep my license. You said—"

"I know what I said. I didn't expect you to get on board that quickly."

"You're right. No sense denying it."

"You need a side project. You need to make it clear that you're not working. With the injunction in play, Brandon's wet dream is to find out you're still in business."

"I haven't opened my studio in weeks."

"I don't mean 'temporarily closed,' or 'finishing up this job that's almost done,' and I don't mean clients-under-the-table either. And yes, I know you've been booking clients under the table."

This was the problem with enlisting the help of a woman who owned an independent surveillance company.

I didn't say anything at first. I slipped on and tied each of my sneakers and let the silence balloon to fill the locker room. A ninety-year-old woman who was a regular swimmer at the pool came in and waved and then went into a dressing stall to change.

It went against everything inside me to take counsel from another person when it came to my business, but a tiny voice in my head knew Nasty was right.

I sat down and turned to her. "Okay, say I take up a side project as you suggest. What happens next?"

She nodded once in acknowledgment of the decision I'd made. "Mad for Mod won't take in any income. Brandon can't claim you're damaging his livelihood. He'll be forced to do business as usual, and that'll isolate how he does that business. We need him to slip up. We need him to show, without any push from us, that his business practices are what led to him losing the job at By George, and as long as he's focused on catching you, he won't make any mistakes."

"That's it? I pretend to give up the one thing that matters to me, and that strengthens our case?"

Nasty stood up and faced me. "No, Madison, that's not it. You have to actually give it up. The furthest thing on your mind will be your company, your finances, and this case. You need to avoid seeing people who work in the decorating business. You need to create the illusion of being carefree. Don't you have any friends you can call? Maybe have a lost weekend?"

"My friends all have common interests. That's why they're my friends."

"What about Tex? It wouldn't be the worst thing in the world for you to be there for him."

I stood up too. "You're his ex-girlfriend. I'm not sure your relationship advice is all that welcome."

"Jeez, woman, get with the program. Tex and I were a blip on the radar four years ago. There's a reason my business exploded. People don't trust the police. I'm private sector. My services are bought and paid for, and people know what they're getting when they hand over a check. If you don't want to have Tex's dinner on the table at six-thirty every night, then rent a theme room at a dirty motel."

I narrowed my eyes. "Why is it so important to you that I abandon my shop?"

She sighed. "Because Brandon Montgomery hired somebody to follow you around, and if I'm going to get anything done, I need you to create a diversion."

6

"I'M BEING FOLLOWED?" I ASKED. I PEEKED OVER MY SHOULDER.

The ninety-year-old stepped out of the dressing stall in a red bathing suit and white rubber swim cap with a strap under the chin. If she was a private detective, then Brandon deserved some credit.

"I'm surprised you didn't predict this yourself. It's not a stretch to learn the person suing you might want to find dirt under your fingernails."

Involuntarily, I held my hand out in front of me. "There's no dirt," I said. I dropped my hand to my side. "Under my fingernails or in my life. It's an open book."

Nasty tipped her head to the side in a gesture that seemed to say, "tomato, tomahto."

"What I do, the information a detective can dig up, is out there for whoever wants to find it. I can explain away anything his guy finds."

"Maybe you can, but you can't control how it's presented.

You've been involved in some weird situations since moving to Dallas. Isn't a movie being made about the pillow stalkings?"

Four years ago, not far from this very spot, I'd found a dead body under the wheels of my car. The case had gotten national attention, and a team of Hollywood producers had bought the rights from one of the suspects. I tried to ignore the fact that my life was being mined for material, but some days it was more difficult than others.

"I'm not involved in the movie."

"You were the main character in the investigation. The closer that movie comes to being made, the more of a local celebrity you're going to be. I won't sugar coat it. That's not going to help you when it comes to character assessment." She turned to face me. "Madison. We've had this conversation. You keep telling me you're open to change, but I don't see it. I've known you for four years. How different is your life now from then?"

"Light years."

"When you met me, I was on the bad-boy roller coaster. I worked for the Lakewood Police Department, got no respect from my peers, and thought you were my competition. Now I make money in my sleep." She put her hand on her belly. "I made six figures the first quarter of this year. My life has changed so much that I'm pregnant and voluntarily helping you with your legal problems. *That's* what happens when you're not opposed to change."

"When we first met, I lived in an apartment. Now I live in a house. I drive a different car. I'm dating a different man."

"You sold that apartment building, and you bought it back. You used to drive an Alfa Romeo, and now you drive, what's that parked outside? Oh yeah. A different Alfa Romeo. As far as men go, using the word "dating" to describe what you've got going with Tex is a stretch. I thought you'd be living together by now. Even though you and I never got along, you always impressed me as a risk-taker. I guess I was wrong."

Nasty's jabs felt like pricks from a voodoo doll, sharp and hot and straight to my most vulnerable spots. I'd been emotionally closed off when I first moved from Pennsylvania to Dallas, and the last thing on my mind had been the possibility of a relationship. More than once since then I'd questioned my choices and felt the pain of the past and the fear of the future. I might not be able to rattle off my lifestyle changes like bullet points on a resume, but I was on the right track. Nasty's opinion of me was the least of my problems.

"You're not wrong," I said.

"Okay. Then find yourself a project that has nothing to do with decorating," she reiterated. "The sooner the better."

"What about my clients?"

"They can wait."

Nasty stood and stretched her arms above her. She tipped her head back. Her spine made a concave curve mirrored in the convex swell of her pregnant belly. Her hair hung down past her waist. Nasty's sexiness struck me the first time I met her, but her pregnancy had brought about something new. A different confidence, one rooted in softness and not aggression. She was still the don't-underestimate-me woman I'd tussled with in the past, but it was less in-your-face.

When she finished her stretch, she dropped her arms and draped her hair over one shoulder. She picked up her handbag and turned toward the exit. She bent down before she left and picked something blue off the floor. She stared at it for a moment and then raised her right foot and checked the red sole of her stiletto pump. She lowered her foot and shrugged.

"What's wrong?" I asked.

"Nothing. I had something stuck to my shoe." She tossed the item into the trash and left.

I went directly to the trash bag and peered in, confirming my suspicions. The object Nasty tracked into the locker room was a midnight-blue rose petal like the one I'd found at the park last night.

7

THE POSSIBILITY EXISTED THAT I, NOT NASTY, HAD BEEN THE ONE to track the rose petal into the locker room. After all, I'd been around rose petals like this last night. But Nasty's response hadn't been one of surprise or confusion or curiosity. She'd tossed the petal as if it were a mild curiosity but nothing more.

Unlike Tex, I wasn't equipped with evidence bags, but instead of tossing the petal, I erred on the side of caution. I set it on a paper towel and folded the towel gently. I had no idea what clue, if any, could be determined from it, but that wasn't for me to decide. I rested the bundle inside my handbag on top of my wallet, pulled a white bell hat that was covered in silk flower petals over my damp hair, and left.

I'd left Wojo and Rocky at home with Tex. While Rocky usually spent the day with me, having the two dogs sometimes left me unnecessarily distracted. While unencumbered by canines, I called my friend Connie Duncan and made plans to meet at a coffee shop.

Connie was a former client who'd become a friend. She and

her husband, Ned, had hired me to design an atomic kitchen, and I'd surpassed their expectations. For a brief period, her husband hit it off with my ex, but both men were now out of the picture. In Connie's case, it was an extramarital affair at a music convention that led to her being separated. She filed for divorce, and despite her husband's apologies and vow to be better, she declared she was moving on.

Connie had been envious over what I'd built with Mad for Mod, and in a fit of inspiration that nobody saw coming, she started an Etsy business for custom sleeves for collectible record albums. She tapped into a hipster market, and when demand surpassed supply, she came to me for help. I offered a corner of my showroom, which she used until the lawsuit forced me to shutter my doors. Now Connie's business was a casualty of the Brandon Montgomery war too.

My lawyer had argued that the businesses weren't connected and Connie should be allowed to continue to use the space, but we'd never formalized our arrangement with rent or a paper trail, and our friendship became the sticking point. Brandon insisted I'd use Connie as a cover to continue work, and the courts agreed. We were granted a two-hour window to move her operation; apparently two hours wasn't long enough for me to do any real damage.

Connie was waiting for me in the parking lot outside Mel's Diner. "Hey," she said, somewhat dejected. "I'm glad you called. I'm so depressed, I spent the morning making the blender go up and down in the kitchen. Probably not the best use of my time."

Ever since Connie's divorce, she'd started experimenting with her personal style. It was as though she were rediscovering who she was without the filter of wife. When we first met, she'd leaned heavily on rockabilly sensibilities, but lately, she was going through a classic rock T-shirt stage. Today the logo was Rolling Stones, paired with oversized jeans that were held up with a thick studded belt. Despite the heat, she wore black patent leather Dr. Martens boots that laced up past her ankles.

When I designed her atomic kitchen, I'd used *The Glass Bottom Boat* as my inspiration. In the movie, Rod Taylor plays an astronaut with a space-age kitchen that delights—and then frustrates—Doris Day. I'd always loved how the appliances were recessed below the surface of the counters and had found a way to replicate the effect through die-cut Formica and hydraulics. I feared if Connie continued to use them as entertainment, the system would break and we'd both be out of luck.

"We should set a date to get your supplies out of my showroom," I said. "At least that way you can work from home."

She frowned. "That's why I'm depressed. Someone posted a bunch of negative reviews—something about the archival paper that I use being too rough for the record surface—a bunch of crap if you ask me, but sales have been on a steady decline ever since."

"Do we know the identity of this mysterious reviewer?"

"Do we need to? Ned's in the music business. He used to recommend my sleeves to clients. Without him spreading the world to the music community, I either have to invest in ads or find a real job."

"Hey," I said, with my finger pointing at her face. "That was a real job. You were a self-employed businesswoman."

"And I've got the Schedule C to prove it."

A waitress came by, and we ordered two coffees and a cheese Danish. The order arrived less than a minute later, and Connie cut the Danish in half and bit into her portion.

"What are we going to do?" she asked with her mouth full. "You're about to lose your business, and mine barely got off the ground." She scanned the interior of the diner. "Maybe I should get a job here. I'll get a uniform that says 'Alice.' Ellen Burstyn could be my Doris Day! Except there's the whole *Exorcist* thing." She pointed at the menu. "Look! They have split pea soup. Didn't they use split pea soup as a prop in *The Exorcist?* It's a sign." She waved to our waitress. "You think they're hiring?"

I put my hand on her forearm. "Connie, maybe you should take a step back and think about what you want out of life. You're going to be on your own. Nobody to tell you what you can and can't do. Dream big!"

"Maybe working at Mel's Diner *is* dreaming big."

I removed my hand. "If working at Mel's Diner is your big dream, then you should go for it."

Behind her, two men sat at a table, loudly complaining about the ratio of egg to cheese in their omelets.

"Maybe I should keep looking," she said.

We finished the Danish and coffee while I filled Connie in on the recent developments with the lawsuit. I hadn't given much thought to our seating choices when we entered the diner, but it occurred to me that I should have sat facing the door so I'd know if someone were watching us. I twisted in my seat and stared out the window.

"Is your back okay?" Connie asked.

"My back?"

"You twisted yourself like you had to crack your back. Did you sleep funny? Or did you and Captain Allen—"

"It's not my back," I said quickly. I readjusted in my chair and faced her. "There's a chance that on top of everything else, I'm now being followed. I didn't think about it when we sat down, but I should probably be more aware of my surroundings and get in the habit of sitting with a view of the parking lot."

Connie waved to get the waitress's attention and pointed at her coffee mug. "Don't worry," she said to me. "None of those people are watching you. They're all coming and going from the florist across the street. Must be a lot of upcoming weddings or something."

We went silent while the waitress poured steaming coffee into our mugs. I added two creamers to cool it off. "Why do you say that?"

"There's been like ten people who came and went and nobody left with anything. I figure they're all there for ideas. You'd think at least one of them would have bought something."

I turned back around and stared at the florist across the street. "You said people have gone in?"

"Sure. It's like Grand Central Station over there."

With nothing to occupy my mind except for Tex's minimal clues, I seized the opportunity to explore something different. "You know, fresh flowers might be just the thing to perk us up. How about we check them out?"

I didn't tell Connie about the midnight-blue rose petals from last night or this morning. For all I knew, that was the latest trend in horticulture couture. But a rose petal seemed to indicate a flower arrangement, and who better to ask about flowers than a florist?

We paid and left. Connie requested a job application on the way out but tossed it in the trash bin after walking past an angry man who argued about the temperature of the coffee. The florist was on the other side of Garland Road, and we were separated from it by two lanes of traffic. In the interest of not signaling exactly where I was at every moment of the day, I hopped into Connie's car and left mine in the diner lot. Less than a minute later, we were in the parking lot across the street.

Akins Flowers was a modest white stucco building with a handful of parking spaces in the front and additional parking out back by their selection of potted plants. Both lots were empty. The windows to the main building were covered with slatted blinds on the inside, turned to minimize sunlight. I understood the challenge they faced; letting sunlight in drove the temperature up, but closing the blinds gave off an unwelcome vibe.

We went inside. Classical music played at a low volume. Mingling with the faint scent of fresh flowers and the subtle yellow and green abstract murals on the walls, it created an ambiance that befitted a florist.

"Where are the employees?" I asked.

"Somebody needed a bathroom break," Connie said knowingly. She approached the refrigerated cases alongside the store. "You want daisies, right? They have yellow with yellow centers, white with yellow centers, pink with white centers, pink with yellow centers—"

"Don't worry about mine. Start thinking about what you want. My treat."

While Connie pressed her nose against the cool glass doors, I wandered to the counter. Behind it, stems of blue roses lay scattered next to butcher paper and a wall-mounted row of colored ribbon. The petals on the freshly cut flowers had curled and wrinkled from lack of water, and a few had fallen off and now rested on the floor.

"Hello?" I called. No one answered.

I pulled my cell phone out and opened the camera app then tapped video and held my phone up. The zoom feature pixelated the image too much, so after looking around a second time, I moved behind the register to peek around more closely. These roses hadn't been abandoned by an employee who had an urgent need for a bathroom break. They'd been left in the open air long enough to turn brown. As I stepped past the register, my hip bumped the mouse and the monitor woke up, displaying an invoice.

From my new position, I hit record and slowly turned in a circle. I held my phone steady and scanned it past the flower arrangement, the discarded flower clippings, the spools of ribbon, and the front counter. When I finished my full rotation, I put my phone away and called out a second time. "Hello? Is anyone here?"

Connie joined me. "Is there a bell? There's usually a bell." She stood on her tiptoes and leaned over the counter then whacked her palm repeatedly on a silver bell next to the register. "Funny place to keep it."

I was growing more and more confident that the employee who'd been working on the floral arrangement had long since left the building—probably not by choice. The dead flowers on the counter and the steady stream of patrons coming in and out both spoke to an unthreatening environment. "Stay here," I told Connie. "I'm going to look for someone out back."

"Okay," she said. She grabbed the bell and moved it to the top of the counter. As I left through the side door, she slapped the bell four more times in swift succession. By the time I returned, I expected her to have written a song.

I exited onto a small stretch of concrete that connected the storefront to the nursery. To the right of the nursery sat rows of potted plants that were showing the effects of too much sunlight. The leaves were yellow. I approached the pots and pressed my fingertips onto the soil. It was dry as a bone.

Despite my sense that something was wrong, aside from overexposure, I had nothing definitive to report. Misters aimed fine moisture at my head, and a cool temperature gave me a chill.

What outside seemed like negligence was not an issue in here. I walked past a table filled with rosemary and oregano plants, to tomatoes, to more sizeable spider plants that had run amok. The same music that I'd heard inside the showroom played out here, and about two-thirds of the way into the nursery, I located a boombox and a CD titled "Classical Music Inspired by Flowers." The playback was set on repeat.

Was I imagining things? This could very easily be one overworked employee who split his or her time between the front desk and the back. Dallas sun and heat claimed photosynthetic organisms quickly, but a crisis might have made the dead plants a byproduct of someone's need to leave in a hurry. As far as I could tell, everything inside the nursery appeared as a nursery should look.

I left the music station and wandered to the back. Taller trees were lined up: Ficus, Areca Palm, and my favorite, Dracaena. I stopped to admire the blade-like green leaves. The name, translated from the original "drakaina," meant female dragon. They were found in the yard of many a mid-century modern house, reflecting more of a trend from that era than any similarity of tastes amongst homeowners. I thought about getting one for Tex when I noticed a partially spilled bag of potting soil on the ground behind the trees.

I leaned to the side and peered at it more closely. It was a twenty-pound bag, torn open and dumped onto the concrete floor. The loose soil was dark and moist. I kicked the toe of my sneaker through the soil to spread it out, but it appeared to be stuck to the ground. I stooped between the potted plants, scooped up a handful, and let it run between my fingers. The dirt left a trace of red on my hand.

I remained paralyzed for a split second while my brain

converted the color of the residue to the likelihood that the residue was blood. I stood quickly and stabilized myself on the closest table, then pulled my phone out of my pocket. I hit Call Back on Tex's most recent call and closed my eyes while waiting for him to answer.

"Captain Allen," he answered.

"It's me. I'm at the flower shop on Garland Road, and I need you to join me."

"Night, I've got a full plate right now. Are you okay?"

"That depends on your definition of okay. I think I found your crime scene."

8

WHILE I WAITED FOR TEX TO ARRIVE, I WENT OUT FRONT TO CHECK on Connie. She'd placed four dozen bud roses on the counter and was sorting through a discount bin of small white teddy bears.

"You have to leave," I said.

"Why? Did you find the owner?"

"I don't think the owner is here."

"Figures," she said. She put the teddy bears back in their basket. "You think I can leave cash on the counter? I like the flowers I picked out."

"Connie, I think you should find another florist." I waited, hoping she'd pick up on my understandably vague anxiety. "Captain Allen is on his way here."

"If you guys want to pick up some rose petals for later tonight—"

"Connie, I beg of you not to finish that sentence."

For the first time since I'd returned from the back room, she seemed to notice my appearance. The misters had left my hair damp, and the short walk to the storefront had left it flat. I knew

46

the blood on my palm was evidence, so as much as I wanted to, I hadn't wiped it off. I took off my hat and fanned my face. My blue-and-white top and blue skirt, like my hair, was plastered to my body.

"Madison, you don't look so hot. Are you sure you want Captain Allen to see you like that?"

The door to the shop opened, and Tex walked in. "Ms. Duncan, I'm going to need you to wait out front while I talk to Ms. Night."

"If I believed for a second that you two were into role play, this would be a little weird." She pushed the door open and walked to her car.

"I'll call you tomorrow," I called after her. She turned around and waved, and then got into her car and drove away.

Tex stared after her for a moment longer than I expected. When he turned back, I jumped right in. "The place was empty but unlocked. It seems like no one's been here for a few days. I scooped up a handful of potting soil from the floor of the nursery out back and…" I held my hand up instead of finishing my sentence.

"Potting soil isn't red," he said.

"No, it isn't."

He pulled an evidence bag out of his pocket and handed me a piece of cloth. "Wipe your hand off with that and then place the cloth in the bag. Seal it. Don't worry about prints. There's no way to keep your DNA from the sample."

I took the bag. After putting the cloth in the bag, I pulled the self-sealing tab and folded the edge over the plastic to keep the sample from becoming contaminated. Tex held a brown paper grocery bag open, and I placed the plastic bag inside it.

"I started to get suspicious when I saw the cut flowers behind the counter. They're blue roses, like the petals we found near the body last night."

"Could mean something, or it could mean the victim ordered flowers."

I pointed behind the counter. "The flowers have been there a few days. Look at the browning on the edges of the petals. And follow me."

I led Tex out the side door past the potted plants and shared my observations about the yellowed leaves and the dry soil. Tex nodded as if he was taking it all in. We got to the nursery, and the cool air and the misted water caused me to shiver. I'd been in and out of the greenhouse twice now, and the juxtaposition of the cool, damp air with the outside humidity left me dizzy. I put one hand on the wooden table for balance, and Tex reached forward and moved my hand off.

"Don't touch anything."

"Sorry. I'm woozy from the heat and the cold."

He intertwined his fingers with mine. Of the two of us, I was the one with calluses. "Hold onto me instead."

This was the first crime scene I'd walked with Tex after we started dating, and while there was no way I could possibly describe it as romantic, I felt a swelling of emotion from deep within me. Tears welled up in my eyes, and I fought against blinking to keep them from falling onto my cheeks. I considered trying to pass my reaction off as a menopausal mood swing, but there were too many legitimate reasons for me to cry to play this off to hormones.

"I'm ... I ..."

Our eyes locked. "Me, too," he said and squeezed my hand.

I wanted to smile, but the scent of rotting tomato reminded me of where we were and why. I turned away and led him behind the row of Dracaena plants where the potting soil bag lay partially open. "There." I pointed to the ground. "I don't know why I ran my hand through it."

"You're a tactile person. It wasn't an odd impulse. Tell me what went through your head right before you touched it."

"The dirt looks moist. That shouldn't mean anything, but it stood out to me. I guess because everything else is dry—the plants outside and the cuttings behind the counter—but this dirt looked wet. Like coffee grounds."

Tex stooped down and used a small brown paper envelope as a spade. He scooped up a sample of the soil and poured it into a plastic bag, sealed the bag, and placed it into his grocery bag of evidence. He stood up and walked to the back of the nursery, where he poked the end of a pen at the wall. His eyes followed the seam of the wall down to the ground. He stared at the ground for a few seconds and then beckoned for me to join him.

"See that?" he said, pointing to two partially visible scrapes on the ground that disappeared by the base of the wall.

"Heel marks?" I guessed.

"Appears that way."

"What does it mean?"

"Means somebody left here against their will."

9

"WHERE'S YOUR CAR?" TEX ASKED.

"Across the street at the diner."

He peeled two plastic evidence bags off his dwindling stack and held them out to me. "Check the bottoms of the boots you wore last night. See if there's anything caked on. The rain destroyed the site, but it would help to get a soil sample to compare back to this." He shook his head. "Of all the things I thought about leaving at your place, evidence bags didn't even make the list."

"We'll talk about that list later." I took the bags. "Do I need a cover story? For why I was here, why my DNA is on the evidence, you know, the works?"

"I'll handle it," he said. At my confusion, he added, "With the truth, Night. This is an open investigation, and your name is already in the case file. Just because I asked you to keep the details to yourself doesn't mean I'm going to muddy an investigation by trying to hide your presence."

"I didn't think you would."

Tex's swift arrival allowed me to walk him through what I'd seen, and that made things easier. I knew there would be questions, but a whole parade of people had come and gone from the flower shop before Connie and I arrived, and their fingerprints would be on the place too. It wasn't until that moment that I understood how difficult Tex's job was about to become.

I drove home.

The dogs were asleep on the sofa. My red rain boots were where I'd left them, on the floor inside the solarium. I picked one up. Tex's suspicion had been right. Clumps of dirt and grass that had dried on now fell in piles on the indoor/outdoor carpeting. Dark-blue rose petals were embedded in the caked-on dirt.

I checked my other boot for more evidence. A tiny cream ribbon was matted in the mud. I extracted it, getting dirt under my fingernails in the process. I flattened the ribbon out on the counter. There was a faint impression of words that had been rubbed off. I held the ribbon taut between my fingers and tilted it toward the light but, aside from a "P", couldn't read what it said.

I'd seen ribbon like this, a row of it, hanging from the workstation at the flower shop—I was sure of it.

I hadn't told Tex about making a video of the interior of the flower shop with my phone, and now that he was at the flower shop, he'd most likely make his own. To be safe, I connected my phone to the computer and emailed a copy of mine to Tex.

Once the email was sent, I disconnected my phone and cued up the video on the monitor. When I made the video, I knew something at the shop wasn't right, but I hadn't begun to realize how wrong "not right" was. By the time I made it to the back of the nursery and discovered the spilled potting soil, I'd forgotten all about the storefront and what evidence I might have seen.

The video opened on the counter behind the register. Long-stemmed roses with formerly dark-blue rose petals were scattered across the surface. The curled and browning petals were easy to see, as were the spools of ribbon on the wall. I zoomed into the view of the ribbon and saw different things printed on each: Happy Birthday on pale blue, Happy Anniversary on red, Thank You on green, Congratulations on black, and Rest In Peace on cream. The tail of the cream ribbon hung longer than the others, as if it had been pulled and not yet rewound.

I zoomed back out and let the video play. As my shaky camera took in the space behind the counter, I scanned three cups filled with pens, pencils, and scissors, a paper cube with an illegible logo, and a turquoise stapler. The screen darkened, and it took me a moment to realize why.

When I'd first bumped the mouse, the monitor had woken and displayed the invoice. I hadn't thought much about it at the time. It stood to reason that a flower shop would have orders coming in and invoices to send out. The presence of cut flowers lying on the counter in mid-arrangement indicated that whoever had been in the shop had been in the middle of a job.

I clicked back ten seconds and watched the video again, this time staring at the monitor. The screen capture was like a giant white rectangle. I paused the video and zoomed to try to see what business had been interrupted by whatever it was that had happened. It was an invoice from Akins Funeral Home and Mortuary.

Akins. Same as the name of the florist.

I grabbed my phone and searched on the name. The mortuary address was familiar. I opened the map app and zoomed in on the address and saw why. Akins Funeral Home and Mortuary sat on the other side of the White Rock Lake picnic area where I'd found the first body.

It wasn't a stretch to think a scrap of ribbon could have escaped their waste management bin or blown off of a grave, gotten caught by a breeze, and ended up by the picnic area. It wasn't a stretch to believe the rose petals had followed a similar fate.

It wasn't a stretch, but it *was* curious. Especially when both businesses shared the same name.

I had an idea. I put the rose petal and clumps of dirt in an evidence bag and slipped the cream ribbon into an envelope. I strongly suspected where they'd originated, but that was because of privileged information. There were a hundred florists in Dallas. A hundred places I could go to order floral arrangements to perk up a room. Any one of them would have various shades of roses in their inventory.

But there was a side entrance to the flower business that I could enter: By George, the wedding and party planning business named in the lawsuit. While working there, I'd overheard the staff members consulting with clients on flower arrangements, so I knew they knew something about roses. I'd stayed away from them the moment Brandon's legal team served me with papers. Perhaps it was time for a social call.

<hr>

I LET the dogs out for a quick potty break, but the oppressive heat left them sluggish and not in the mood to play. Rocky left a deposit by the corner of the garden, and Wojo lifted a leg on a tomato plant. It was two o'clock. I locked the dogs back inside the air conditioning and headed out to the one place I probably shouldn't have gone in the first place.

By George was one of the biggest wedding planners in the city. Unlike the budget planners around town, George kept a staff of consultants and business accounts at bakeries, florists, and bridal salons in Dallas. And like Nancy Drew's best friend, George was a woman.

I drove into downtown Dallas and parked at a meter a few blocks from the Historic West End arch. It was a brick fixture rigged with neon words announcing the spot to the tourists who made it a destination. When I first moved to the city, I spent a day wandering the area, touring the Texas Book Depository sixth-floor museum and the accompanying Kennedy memorial with eternal flame, but aside from the century-old brick warehouses that had been converted into living quarters, my work renovating mid-century properties kept me from this part of the city.

By George took up the better part of a city block. The main building housed an office and showroom, both of which were part of the job I'd inherited from Brandon's neglect. George was the consultant of choice for debutantes and big-budget weddings, and she wanted an impressive showroom for potential clients. It would have ranked among my more fun projects if the design had originated with me, but at the time she'd been auditioning designers, I'd still been small potatoes.

Already the heat was dictating people stay inside for the day. I entered the showroom and allowed cool, crisp air to envelop me, then fluffed my ashy-blond hair with my fingertips, smoothed out my skirt, and spotted George carrying a potted orchid to the front desk.

George was an attractive, middle-aged woman who'd recently lost her husband to an unexpected heart attack. Instead of selling the bridal shop when he died, she took the money from the insurance payout and invested it into expansion and redesign. It was rare to meet people who loved their jobs as much as George did, and I'd been grateful that circumstances had allowed me to be part of her plans. I'd completed the job quickly and under budget and assumed that combination earned me a welcome greeting despite the circumstances.

George's eyes widened when recognition hit. She dropped the orchid. I heard a thud as the clay pot landed on the rubber mat that covered the floor. George bent down to retrieve the plant and set it back on the counter.

"Madison," she called out in greeting. "I didn't expect to see you today. This isn't about the lawsuit, is it? My deposition is tomorrow, and I don't think—"

"I'm here for a social call," I said quickly. There seemed no point making her feel guilty over the drama Brandon had initiated. "You look busy."

She was relieved. "We are. The expansion allowed us to create a consignment shop for heirloom bridal accessories. Vintage is the biggest trend now. Millennials want to minimize their carbon footprint, and there's nothing like a one-of-a-kind veil from the twenties to satisfy both mom and daughter." She closed the appointment book and rested her pen, a long, pearly-white instrument with a fluff of marabou on the end, diagonally across the top. "I've already booked four brides and a coming-out party this month."

"That's great news. Exactly what you were hoping for."

"None of this would have happened if you hadn't stepped in and met the original completion date for the renovation. I'm going to tell the court that, too."

"I appreciate that," I said truthfully. Having an endorsement from the client at the center of the lawsuit had to help my case. I reached into the inside pocket of my handbag and pulled out the creamy satin ribbon. "I'm here about this. I think it was used on an arrangement with dark-blue roses." I feigned ignorance. "Maybe a wedding? I was hoping you might recognize it."

George took the ribbon and flattened it out on the counter between us. "Every wedding planner in the country keeps ivory satin ribbon on hand, but this wasn't used for a wedding."

"How can you tell?"

"There's writing on here." She put on a pair of glasses that had been resting on the table and peered closer at the ribbon. "It looks like it was rubbed off. Look." She pulled the ribbon taut like I had and held it toward me. I put on my readers and then squinted at the ribbon.

"These were from a funeral arrangement," she said. "The words are stamped on with gold heat stamp. 'Rest in Peace.' I'd say that was on a grave and the hot Dallas sun bleached it out." She handed the ribbon to me. "I hope that doesn't creep you out."

I refrained from telling her how I'd come to be in possession of the ribbon. There was creepy, and then there was *creepy*. "I was more curious about the flowers than the ribbon. They were dark-blue roses. I've never seen roses that shade of blue."

"I'm not surprised. They're not bred to be that color. Most florists prefer to focus on what occurs in nature and not what they can create in a lab."

I didn't have a chance to ask more questions. The door behind me opened, and a Texas drawl greeted us. "Well, well. Today must be my lucky day."

It was a voice I heard in my nightmares. I turned around and found myself face to face with Brandon Montgomery.

"MADISON NIGHT, AS I LIVE AND BREATHE," BRANDON SAID. "I don't suppose you're here to influence George's deposition, are you? Or doing business on the sly? Looking for leads? Maybe you're going to be a wedding planner and are trying to steal *her* files."

Brandon Montgomery was a mousey man who dressed in gingham checked shirts, paisley bowties, expensive jeans, and sneakers that were bright white. I suspected as soon as a pair showed signs of wear, he tossed them and unboxed the next. His hair stuck straight up thanks to an aggressive styling product. He had close-set eyes and a turned-up nose, both of which made him look younger than forty, his actual age.

"Brandon," I said coolly. "Nice to see you. I was here to place an order." I turned to George. "I'd like two dozen Gerbera daisies for delivery," I said. "They're for me personally. I don't need them by a specific date, but I would like them earlier rather than later."

George woke up her computer and typed something. "Two dozen Gerbera daisies. Looks like I can add that to another order and have them ready by the end of the week. Did you want a vase?"

"Box delivery is fine. I have a few vintage vases at home that I'd love to put to good use."

"Box it is."

George repeated my order back to me and, when I confirmed it, moved to the register. I suspected she was crossing her Ts and dotting her Is as much as I was thanks to Brandon's presence. George had been supportive of me through all of this, and the last thing I wanted was to do something that cast her in a negative light.

I paid for the order and left, refraining from wishing her luck with her deposition in front of Brandon.

He followed me onto the sidewalk. "Nice try, Madison. I know what you're up to."

I kept walking. "Good. Then you understand why I was willing to risk running into you to meet with George."

"She's not your client. You stole that account out from under me, and now you're trying to pilfer leads that should have been mine. Everybody knows the best clients are the ones that come from word of mouth. And you're not even clever about it!"

I spun to face him with my fists balled in frustration. "I didn't steal your account. You abandoned that job halfway through, and I was hired to finish it."

Brandon's face turned red. "You're the worst kind of designer. You're unoriginal."

"Is *that* the worst?" I asked with feigned innocence. "I would have thought the worst was the one who walks off a job and leaves the client in the lurch. Silly me."

He leaned forward and pointed his finger at me. "By the time

I'm through with you, you'll be lucky to decorate fire halls." He turned away and stormed back into the wedding shop.

Brandon's animosity toward me was so over the top, I was tempted to treat him like a whiny child. And I had, at first. But his criticism hit a tender spot that wasn't without truth.

When his legal team identified my method of relying on inspiration from Doris Day movies to conceive of rooms for my mid-century-loving clients, they held it up as an example of my tendency to copy what had already been done instead of demonstrating true creativity. Overnight, the quirk that was my strength became my biggest weakness.

I walked to my car, shrugged out of my blue-and-white blazer, and tossed it on the passenger seat. I ran the air conditioner and cooled down. I'd hoped to get a lead from George, but Brandon's unexpected appearance interrupted me. How had he known I'd be at the flower shop? That was the last place I should have been. Nasty had warned me that I was being followed. I needed to pay better attention.

It was odd not having a destination. I drove north on a combination of highways and side streets, taking two random exits without signaling first. It was a small act of defiance against the growing sensation that until the lawsuit was settled, I had no daily purpose. I wondered if the court would grant me damages for that.

After a circuitous route that included the greater Dallas area, I drove home. There was a note on the kitchen table asking me to call Tex, so I did.

"Allen," he answered.

"It's me," I said. "I just got home, and we seem to be down one canine. Please tell me you have Wojo."

"I have Wojo. I also have bad news. When I came by to get him, a reporter was hanging around your place. He said he's working on a follow-up story about you and wants a quote."

"My relationship with the press is somewhat contentious these days," I said. "You can throw out his contact information. I'm not going to call him back."

"Night, there's a possibility that this isn't about Doris Day or the lawsuit. It could be about my case. I didn't think anybody knew you were at the lake with me, but we didn't try to hide it. If somebody leaked your name as being the one who found the body, you might be in for some additional harassment."

"You need me to talk to them, don't you?" It was a question, but my voice fell flat as I asked it.

"I need you to dodge them. Until I know what I'm looking at, I'd like to control what gets leaked to the public."

DODGING the press meant staying away from home. The oppressive Dallas temperatures weren't fun for a dog, but riding around in a car was. I secured Rocky in his car seat and cracked the window. He aimed his nose at the air. He looked so cute that I pretended not to mind the rain that dampened the passenger seat until I started fearing for my car's interior. I rolled up the window, and Rocky whimpered. I drove aimlessly, eventually pulling onto the narrow gravel road around White Rock Lake.

The rain that started when Tex and I were at the picnic area had remained consistent as Dallas rain often did. We were in for a week of showers that were neither tempestuous nor cool. It kept visitors away from what would otherwise be a midday picnic spot. It was slow going over the wet, unpaved gravel, and twice my wheels spun when they caught in a muddy pothole. I didn't expect to do much more than drive in a loop around the lake, but when I reached the pavilion, I pulled off the road and parked.

The closer I'd gotten to the pavilion, the more I expected to find reporters or civilians, or possibly even a police officer stationed to keep people out. My expectations weren't met. The pavilion and the parking lot were both empty. I unclipped Rocky's car seat, and he stood up and shook his fur.

I knew what I was doing. Keeping myself busy with questions regarding an investigation that had nothing to do with me instead of stopping to think what would happen if I lost everything I'd worked so hard to build. I'd convinced myself that going to By George was an innocent excursion, but it wasn't.

I hadn't talked to George since the papers were served, and I wanted her to tell me that I hadn't done anything wrong. I wanted her to say I gave her what she wanted, not what Brandon designed or that the renovation had successfully contributed to her bottom line. But the truth was, I was new to the world of business renovations, and picking up the slack that Brandon left behind had been the path of least resistance. I might not have agreed with the concept he'd pitched to George, but she'd bought it. That was what she'd wanted.

But there was truth behind the insults Brandon slung at me. I'd watched Doris Day's movies, sometimes on repeat when I needed a pick-me-up or to feel a connection to a family life I barely remembered. I couldn't say what I came up with myself or lifted from an existing design created for Universal Studios sixty years ago.

Worse than the accusations were the self-doubts. Maybe I was using what I'd seen in a movie or a back issue of *Better Homes and Gardens*. Maybe I didn't have an original bone in my body. Maybe Brandon was right.

Rocky crawled over my lap and put his paws on the inside window. He pressed his nose to the glass and left a smudge in the condensation. After a few whimpers, I acquiesced and clipped on his leash. I opened the door, and he jumped out, directly into a puddle.

I got out of the car and waited while he relieved himself by a small patch of overgrown grass. When he finished, he pulled me toward the pavilion. I didn't much mind the rain, and I owned enough pairs of Keds that having this pair get saturated through the canvas to my foot wasn't a problem. The rubber soles were slippery against the slick grass blades, but I walked slowly until we were under the sloped roof.

Eight picnic tables, flanked by benches, sat under the pavilion. The concrete underfoot was dry except for a puddle in the center courtesy of a leak in the roof. I lowered myself onto a bench and rested my head on my hands. I couldn't shake the feeling that things—the world around me—was changing, and if I didn't get on board, I'd be left behind. Even Nasty had made it clear she believed I lived in the past. I'd always attributed that to my business, but if I lost that business and had to start over, would I do things differently? Or was she right: was I destined to continue repeating the past while everyone around me experienced something new?

I watched as Rocky sniffed the puddle under the table. A fat droplet fell on top of his head, and he shook it rapidly. Another droplet hit his nose, and he backed away a few steps. I kept my eyes on him and paid little attention to the fact that what started as one and then two droplets turned into a steady leak until a flash of lightning scared me into dropping his leash. Thunder boomed overhead, and Rocky took off for the hedge that separated the picnic area from the mortuary grounds.

"Rocky! Get back here," I demanded.

He slipped through an opening in the fence. I ran out from under the pavilion to the shrubs and squatted into the muddy grass to discover a view of a small, wet puppy seeking shelter while trailing his leash behind him.

I RACED BACK TO MY CAR AND SPUN MY WHEELS ON THE WET pavement in my haste to get to the mortuary. Rocky was a friendly dog with tags and a leash, but he was scared and alone, and so was I.

The minutes that passed while I drove felt like hours. Akins Funeral and Mortuary had an impressive entrance on the northwest side of White Rock Lake. I drove through the downpour, around the lake, turned right on Peavy, drove a short distance past the park, and eased into a space marked Visitor. Gates to the cemetery were open, and a blue appliance repair van was parked at the other end of the lot.

The tasteful white brick building sat on a manicured green lawn. A sidewalk, interrupted by three concrete stairs, led to the front door. There were no signs of Rocky, but small, rapidly fading wet pawprints were visible on the concrete under the awning. With the rain pelting me, I ran from my car to the entrance and slipped inside the building. The damp followed me, though the inside temperature dropped by about twenty degrees.

Door chimes announced my entry into a small foyer. To my left was a closed door marked Office. To my right were a coat check and a lavatory. And directly in front of me was a waiting room that led to a viewing area. Days-old floral arrangements were lined up in the waiting room. The edges of the roses and carnations used were brown with age. I cared less about the flowers than the small, wet dog cowering under the last chair in a row of foldout seating.

"Rocky! Get out here right now," I whispered urgently.

Rocky quivered and then sank onto his front paws, stuck his butt in the air, and stretched. He came out from under the seat with his head low, like he knew he'd done something wrong. Resistant as I was to his adorableness, I quickly scooped him up and hugged him (which served the secondary purpose of not letting him run away a second time).

As I held Rocky, I took a moment to surveil the room. The walls were dark mahogany wood with a modest mantel that ran the perimeter. Vases with tasteful flower arrangements sat below watercolors of nature scenes. Several rows of cane back chairs had been set up in the room facing the far left. A wreath of white carnations sat next to an empty casket, and a cream satin banner with "Rest in Peace" printed in blue ink was draped diagonally across the arrangement.

When Rocky stopped shivering, I double-checked his leash and then set him on the floor. He sniffed the carpet like a bloodhound following a trail and stretched his leash toward the door. I studied the display of framed photographs. The deceased appeared to have been the patriarch of a large family, and the photos were filled with smiling faces of multiple generations who shared the same freckles and petite nose.

"Excuse me. This room isn't open for viewing," said a voice

from the doorway. I turned slowly and discovered a man with a pudgy build looking at Rocky. He shifted his gaze to me. "I'm going to have to ask you to leave."

I tugged Rocky's leash, and he returned to my ankles. "Forgive us," I said. "I was outside by the park, and the lightning and thunder scared my dog. He disappeared through a hole in the fence, and I found him in here."

The man's narrow shoulders sloped at an angle that even the lines of his suit jacket couldn't correct. Under his jacket, his collar was half up and half down, and his tie was askew. His shoes were not shoes. They were sneakers—as if running a funeral home required him to be ready to make a quick getaway.

A loud boom of thunder clapped overhead. Rocky squatted on the carpet and left a spot.

"Rocky, no!"

He looked up at me, embarrassed and scared and in need of a hug. I pulled a travel-sized package of stain remover towelettes from my handbag and extracted one, then stooped down to the floor and scrubbed at the spot.

The man bent down and ruffled Rocky's fur. "It's okay, little fella. I get scared of the thunder too."

We both stood up.

"We don't get many furry visitors like him." He stood back up and held out his hand. "Arnold Akins," he said.

"Madison Night. This is Rocky."

Arnold smiled. "Poor little guy is scared stiff." He smiled sheepishly. "A little mortuary humor there. Follow me. I can spare a couple of minutes to sit with you until the rain lets up."

The three of us traipsed down a carpeted hallway and turned right into a cluttered office. Inside was a desk opposite two chairs, a globe on a metal stand, and a table covered in a green cloth that held a miniature model of the mortuary grounds. On the walls were a collection of framed photos of plots, headstones, and mausoleums, and above it all was a banner that said, "Akins Mortuary: providing the plot to your next chapter."

Arnold took off his jacket and hung it on the back of his chair. He wore both suspenders and a belt. I settled into the moderately comfortable seat on the opposite side of Arnold's desk. He opened a drawer and extracted a small baggie filled with bite-sized, bone-shaped dog biscuits. He waved the bag in front of Rocky's nose and, when Rocky showed interest in the contents, pulled one out and handed it over.

"Thank you," I said. "He doesn't usually run off like that, and my heart almost stopped when he disappeared through the hedge. I assumed there was a fence or a gate that ran the perimeter of the cemetery."

Arnold's face colored. "There is, but kids these days, they like to get in here after dark and throw zombie parties. It's ridiculous what I find when I take the golf cart around the grounds in the morning. Empty bottles of booze, articles of clothing, you name it. As quickly as the city repairs it, the kids find another place to break it."

"It surprises me that the fence is the city's responsibility," I said casually.

"The land around here's all sliced up. They tried to squeeze us out by raising taxes, but Dad borrowed money from a wealthy businessman and kept us afloat for a while."

"I'm sorry for the questions. I'm a decorator. I tend to work on residential properties, so I haven't had much interaction with the city."

Arnold grunted. "Consider yourself lucky. Getting the city to handle anything is a nightmare. Take that fence, for example. It's been broken for who knows how long, and nobody wants to deal with it. I told my dad—" He stopped abruptly. "Some problems work themselves out, right? I shouldn't complain."

I shifted my attention back to the map of the grounds. "Does the city own all of the property around you?"

Arnold's face darkened. "The city wants to expand the park. We've been holding them off so we can maintain a respectable perimeter for our guests," he said. On the word "guests," he moved his hand and indicated the cemetery plots in the center of the grounds. "We can't do anything about the caliber of people who hang out at the pavilion. They're not supposed to be there after dark, but there's always someone who thinks a graveyard is sexy."

The windows flashed with a pulse of bright light, quickly followed by a boom of thunder. Rocky crowded closer to my ankles and whimpered. A sheet of rain pelted the roof. In the hallway, a door slammed shut, and a male voice muttered under his breath.

Arnold put his hands palm-side down on his desk and watched the door. He didn't seem concerned by the identity of the new arrival, but something in his demeanor changed. A few seconds later, a white-haired man with black glasses, the kind favored by scientists in the fifties, filled the doorway. He wore a canvas fishing hat that dripped from the brim, a tan polo shirt, and similarly colored baggy cargo shorts. His legs were partially covered in white socks pulled halfway up his calves and navy-blue rubber Crocs. The Crocs were shiny from the rainwater. He pulled his glasses off and blinked a few times, wiped the lenses on his shirttails, and put them back on his face.

"Well, Arnold, fire up the incinerator. Acie's on her deathbed, and I think it's time to pull the plug." He rifled through the desk. His hands landed on something hard underneath a stack of paper, and when he moved the papers aside he revealed a hammer. "A-ha! That'll do the trick." His eyes glittered with excitement.

Arnold watched me nervously. "He's talking about the air conditioner," he explained. He put his hand on top of the hammer. "Leave it be, Dad. Quinn's working on her now."

The white-haired man dropped his hands to his waist. His shoulders sloped too, and despite his age, he had the body language of a small child who's been told not to play with his food.

"I say we dig a hole and toss her in like the others." He seemed to see me for the first time. "Are you the new girl?" He turned to Arnold. "Is she the new girl?" Back to me. "I'm Edward."

Edward's use of the word "girl" to describe a fifty-year-old woman had more to do with his generation than my youthful looks, though sunscreen and good genes had left me looking younger than my age.

"This is Madison," Arnold said. "She's a decorator."

"Decorator, you say? Care to decorate the front desk and answer the phones? Maybe schedule a hit on an air conditioning unit?" He waggled his eyebrows, causing me to laugh. "Probably not. That's the problem with you kids today. You all want to be YouTube stars." He turned around and left.

"Don't mind my dad," Arnold said. "He calls everybody 'girl.'"

"Even boys?" I asked with a straight face.

"Especially boys." Arnold smiled, but I suspected his dad's shenanigans left Arnold's day-to-day life slightly more challenging. "I wish I could say that was par for the course, but he's been ten times worse since his bank loan application was rejected."

"I thought you said you had financial help from a wealthy businessman?"

"We did. And two weeks ago, the balloon payment on the loan came due, and Dad didn't have the money. The deed turned over to the new owner, who told the press he was selling the lot to the city."

"BUT PEOPLE ARE BURIED HERE FOREVER," I SAID. "SURELY THE CITY doesn't plan to relocate the bodies."

"No, they don't. Most of our residents have been with us from the beginning. It's up to the family to pay to relocate them, and that isn't the kind of expense you budget for."

"Then what? They'd pave over the grounds?"

"The picnic area by the lake is one of the most popular spots around town, and the city wants to monetize it through expansion. Tennis courts, cooking stations. Double the size of the picnic area, build a concert dome. With the right draw, the parking fees alone could pay the expansion plans off in a year."

"It might be solid business on paper, but even the city planners must understand the repercussions of uprooting the deceased from their final resting place."

"It's hard to say if they do or don't. These dummies understand dollar signs and not a whole lot more."

I took a moment to study the map of the mortuary grounds

and carefully planned cemetery plots. "How long has the mortuary been in your family?" I asked.

"Seventy years. Dad bought the place when he was twenty. He was a gardener. He saw the wealthy families investing in property, and he did the same. As soon as he had a little money saved, he bought the place and changed the name."

"Isn't that an unusual path? I would have thought he'd open a landscaping business."

"Do you know much about the history of funeral homes?"

I admitted that I did not.

"There was a boom in the late nineteenth century into the twenties, so much so that formalized training on embalming and cremation was readily available. Medications helped people live longer too. After the war, families settled down in the suburbs and made homes for themselves. They wanted the white picket fence and the station wagon in the driveway. People wanted roots."

"But a fifteen-hundred-square-foot tract house on a quarter-acre property doesn't allow for a family burial site in the backyard," I surmised.

"See? You know more than you think. Funeral homes became a cottage industry. Casket makers, life insurance companies, and florists all benefitted from a sort of halo effect."

"The flower shop on Garland Road," I said. "Akins. That's you too."

"That was my idea," Arnold said proudly. "Fewer people are coming to us for their burial needs, and if we're going to stay profitable, we need another income stream. I thought it was a good idea to keep some of our business needs in-house."

"Diversification," I said.

Arnold nodded. "About ten years ago, Winston Burr offered to buy the mortuary. Land was cheap back when Dad bought the property, but with the city's plans for expansion, the property values swelled. Dad would have turned him down flat, but I convinced him to take the money to buy the nursery. Winston gave him a loan against the mortuary. The note came due last month, and the deed to the business defaulted to Burr."

It took me a moment to place why the name was familiar. Winston Burr was a developer who'd hit it big by investing in property in the outlying towns of Garland, Frisco, and Plano. He put his first million into the hotel industry and quadrupled his net worth quickly, becoming one of the richest men in Dallas.

I didn't spend a lot of time thinking about how the wealthy residents of Dallas became the wealthy residents of Dallas. Most of them appeared to have long lineages of deep-pocketed families who owned streets, parks, and private art collections that rivaled the museums of mid-sized cities. It was a given that the city had been bought and paid for. I suspected most of the infrastructure had been funded with a check drawn on the family funds. And yet, I doubted it mattered to the city residents who owned what as long as the town was clean, safe, and enjoyable.

The Burrs had been a moderate working-class family, but their youngest son, Winston, came out from the shadows and made possession of property his motivating force. In the eighties, he backed city council members who agreed to his beautification plans and bailed out businesses that teetered on the brink of bankruptcy.

There'd been a stretch of ten years where Dallas was named one of the fastest-growing cities in America, and Winston had put his money into the right thing at the right time. Once he became a millionaire, he bought a mansion in the richest part of the city, not five miles from the epicenter. His house was the highlight of the city bus tour because he was one of their own: a local boy who got rich by seeing something valuable in his backyard. He was the J.R. Ewing of city planning.

But that wasn't where I knew him from. When the city cut police budgets, Tex turned to private donors. Winston had been generous to the police force, keeping them from bankruptcy.

"The same Winston Burr who donated ten million dollars to the police department last year?"

"Yes."

"You don't sound happy about the arrangement."

Arnold's cheeks colored. "We were barely keeping ourselves afloat," he said. "Dad bought this place back when he was young and physically fit. He was able to maintain the grounds in the early morning and meet with new clients during the day. Mom managed the books. I started helping out around here when I was ten." He smiled sheepishly. "It wasn't official until I was sixteen. Child labor laws and whatnot."

"Of course," I said.

"When Mom died, Dad let things go. There's a saying among funeral directors: this is a three-generation business. The first generation starts it, the second generation makes it prosperous, and it dies with the third. I never had kids, so ours is limping along with no real long-term plan."

It was oddly refreshing to talk about the business of death. It wasn't a popular cocktail party topic, but for those of us who profited from it, it was a necessary part of the circle of life. My involvement usually consisted of lifting the burden of estate liquidation from surviving family members.

The mortuary business was more delicate than that. Funeral directors held their clients' hands through myriad choices about the deceased's final resting place. Arnold was no different than others I'd met. He had a gentle manner about him, though I recognized that underneath he was as mercenary as I was when it came to the company balance sheet.

"When did your mother die?" I asked.

"Twenty years ago."

The conversation lapsed, and this time I didn't try to revive it. There was something about losing a parent early in life that brought people together, almost as if we were members of a private club. The pain never went away, but we learned to internalize it and go on. And the hole left behind by the loss of their presence became the thing we tried to fill for the rest of our lives.

Arnold, who'd kept his attention on me since I first walked in, seemed to be distracted by something on his computer. He turned his head toward me, but his eyes remained on the screen. He eased open his desk drawer and felt around with his right hand while his left hand tapped at the down arrow on his keyboard.

"Is everything okay?" I asked.

He seemed to have forgotten I was there. "Sorry." He shook his head rapidly as if trying to clear disturbing thoughts. "It's my dad. He seems like a funny old man, but sometimes it's like being in business with Dennis the Menace."

"What did he do?"

"About a week ago, after he found out he lost the property, he bought a bottle of scotch and went joyriding in the golf cart. The brakes went out, and he crashed into a hedge and slept off his hangover behind a tombstone. Ever since then, I've been dealing with the wreckage."

"Does that happen often?"

"The golf cart?" Arnold sighed. "The brakes go in and out. Dad refused to spend money on getting the cart serviced and did the work himself." Arnold shook his head.

"He wasn't injured, was he?"

"From the golf cart crash? Nah. Dad will outlive us all." Arnold sighed. "But who knows what other damage he did. For all I know, he's the one who broke the air conditioning unit. We both thought selling the place would fix things. Winston said he'd keep us both on in management roles until the city plans are official, but now, I'm working as hard as ever. And since the sale, Dad wants to spend his days fishing."

"Maybe he wants to enjoy his retirement."

He rubbed his forehead. "I watched my dad spend his whole life right here. After he took that loan, things were different. Like he sold off a part of the life he had with my mom. I never wanted to run the mortuary, but I stayed on for him. The way things look now, I might have a chance at a real life after all."

13

I HAD A HARD TIME PUTTING MYSELF INTO ARNOLD'S HEADSPACE. I never would have willingly sold off my decorating business, but now, thanks to the lawsuit, I was at risk of losing it anyway.

The buzzer outside the service entrance rang again, and this time the sound was more insistent. Arnold left his desk and stood in the doorway. "Dad?" he called. There was no answer. He turned back to me. "I'm so sorry. Can you excuse me for a moment?"

"Sure," I said.

Being an interior decorator, I often profiled clients based on the objects they interacted with, and on initial consultations, I always asked them to tell me about a prized possession. It was not seeing a striking vase, painting, bookcase, or record player that told me what they were about but hearing the story behind it. Something picked up from a street corner that served a purpose did not carry the same weight as an object handed down from a previous generation that came infused with memories.

Arnold Akins's office was a study in hand-me-downs. In addition to the mismatched framed photos on the wall and the miniature model of the mortuary grounds, there were two chairs, a stately maple desk, and one black standard-issue office chair behind it. The back wall was covered with shelves that housed a collection of decorative urns, an interesting choice of knickknack considering the business he was in.

His desk was neat. A metal tray contained envelopes, catalogs, and a Farmer's Almanac with colorful Post-Its marking various pages. His wireless keyboard and mouse were carefully placed in front of his monitor. Three silver frames faced the desk chair, visible to the person who occupied the chair.

It was boredom more than sleuthing that led me to lean over the desk to look at the photos. Two men wearing canvas fishing hats, smiling broadly. One held a large catch dangling off a fishing wire. The other held two poles. There was an air of familiarity about the men, and I placed the one with the poles as a younger version of Edward, Arnold's father. I didn't recognize the man on the right.

"You're still here?" asked a voice behind me.

I stood and turned and faced Edward himself. He'd lost the fishing hat, and I could see a stripe of demarcation across his forehead where his tan line ended. He held a long, sharp pair of gardening shears in his hand. The affable old-man act was gone, and in its place was something more menacing.

His arrival startled me. I put my hands on the desk to right myself. My palm landed on the in-basket, the in-basket slid across the desk, and the tray fell, scattering pieces of paper across the carpet. Rocky was quick to sniff them. I bent down and picked up the papers closest to me.

A creased and sun-spotted hand grabbed ahold of my upper arm and lifted me to my feet. "Leave them," Edward said.

I smiled and stepped away from the desk. "I was hoping

Arnold would return before I left. I wanted to give him this." I held out a business card.

Edward took the card and stared at it for a few seconds. "We're not in a position to hire a decorator," he said. He tried to hand the card back, and I refused it.

"I'm not in a position to be your decorator. I'm involved in a lawsuit that has made me temporarily close my business. I have time on my hands. Let me help you out during the day. You mentioned earlier that you hired someone who didn't show when you were talking about the air conditioner. I'm not looking for a full-time job or even a paycheck. I'm looking for something to keep me from going stir crazy. I can manage your books or do odd jobs. Help you set up for services, manage your calendar. Anything you need." An unexpected note of desperation had crept into my voice.

Edward's face softened, and I knew he understood what it was I sought. "Let me hold on to this," he said, raising my card. He tucked it into the pocket of his plaid shirt and patted the fabric.

Despite the finality represented by the cemetery, I exited Akins Funeral and Mortuary with a hopefulness I hadn't felt in over a month. The rain had shifted from an insistent downpour to a steady drizzle that dampened both Rocky and me on the way to the car. The blue appliance repair van had been moved closer to the building and now blocked me in.

A man in a heathered gray T-shirt and khaki work pants came out of the building next door. He had deeply tanned skin and longish gray hair that was kept out of his face with a red canvas visor.

"You must be Quinn," I said.

"Says who?"

I cut my eyes between him and the appliance logo on the side of the van. "You are here to repair the air conditioning, right? Edward mentioned you while I was inside."

"Yeah, I'm Quinn," he said. "Don't get a lot of strangers walking up and calling me by my name. Sorry about the van. I'll get it out of your way." He thrust his hand into his pocket and pulled out a ring that held two dozen keys. He knew exactly which one he wanted and moved the rest out of his way then unlocked the van and climbed inside. A few moments later, the van disappeared around the side of the offices, clearing the exit.

I'd spent the last hour at Akins Funeral Home, but it was Rocky who led me through their door. I had no intent to get involved in Tex's case, yet I felt I'd learned pieces of information that might or might not mean something to him.

There was a break in the fence that connected the mortuary property to the pavilion where the bodies were found. The funeral home next to the pavilion was having financial trouble. And they owned the flower shop that Tex confirmed was a crime scene. Were these connections to the unidentified bodies, or was I simply shoehorning observations into a neat little pattern?

I found my thoughts returning to Akins Flowers. Opening a flower shop allowed the mortuary to serve visitors who wanted to leave something behind. In terms of business diversification, it was a good idea.

It was why I depleted my savings and bought an apartment complex when I first moved to Dallas. I hadn't had a lot of money left after that, but I remained happy with the investment. The rent from my tenants had floated me while Mad for Mod found a loyal client base, and when I sold the building, I made back my investment.

When I bought the building back from the new owner, I took a loss. That's what happens when you make business decisions with your heart and not your head.

I shook off the sense that it was a need for a distraction that led me to the funeral home more than any real belief they were involved in Tex's double homicide, but a growing lack of purpose filled me with the realization that I was lying to myself. Nasty had been the one to suggest I find a hobby, and I doubted Tex would want me to canvas the area on behalf of the police department.

Except he had two victims and no positive identification. He was going to need the public's help. And if Nasty was right, and Brandon Montgomery's people were following me, then I could think of no better way to prove my business was closed than to throw myself into public service instead.

14

IF THERE WAS ONE THING TEX HAD DRILLED INTO MY HEAD IN THE four years we'd known each other, it was that cops, specifically investigators, had resources that I, a layperson, did not. I'd been known to stumble into circumstances and reason my way out, and I'd always contended that I used the same analytical skill set that Tex did despite how and where we'd honed those instincts. But I'd accepted that our efforts were better when combined than not, and not sharing information that could relate to an investigation was as bad as actively withholding it. I drove to the police station.

A pretty woman with strawberry-blond hair stood by the copier behind the front desk. She was dressed in a pink shirt, narrow-legged white pants, and sand-colored ballerina flats. I'd been to the police station more times than I could count, and even with this woman's efficiency, she looked almost as out of place as I did.

"Can I help you?" she asked.

Lately, Officer Garcia had become a reliable fixture behind the desk, and after his unfortunate weapons discharge, it seemed he'd be stationed there indefinitely.

"Where's Officer Garcia?" I asked.

"At home with his kids. Are you a friend?"

"Sort of," I said. "I sometimes help the police."

"That's what I'm doing!" She lowered her voice. "I'm a mystery writer. I had an idea for a police procedural and thought this would be good research. Did you know the human body can live for thirteen seconds after a fatal shot to the heart?" Her eyes were bright with enthusiasm, and I could tell she had no idea this wasn't the type of conversation that would get her invited to dinner parties.

I stifled a smile. Tex often pointed at detective novels and complained about how far from the truth they were. I often pointed out the meaning of the word fiction. I wondered if she'd told him her aspirations during the interview and if that had won her points.

"I'm Imogene," she said. "Are you here with a complaint? Or a case? Maybe you want to confess to something?"

Anonymity felt like a lie of omission. While I was toying with the pros and cons of telling her who I was and why I was there, she grabbed a flyer from the output tray of the copier and handed it to me. "I haven't posted this on the bulletin board yet, but the police captain wants to assemble a volunteer team to canvas the lake for evidence in a double homicide," she said. "It's going to be all over the news."

I took the yellow paper. "Where do I sign up?"

"You don't," said a voice behind me. A familiar voice, the same voice that often argued with me about fiction, police procedurals, and the dirty dishes he sometimes left in my sink. I turned slowly and faced Tex.

He'd changed since this morning and was now was dressed in a white dress shirt and jeans. As the captain, he was expected to wear a suit and tie, but Tex often didn't do what was expected. Before being promoted, he'd earned a solid enough reputation that his loose interpretation of the dress code went unchallenged.

"Captain Allen," Imogene said. "This nice lady wanted to volunteer." She held up a flyer. "I told her about your task force, and she was interested."

Tex kept his eyes trained on me. "Imogene, this 'nice lady' is Madison Night."

"Oh," Imogene said. *"Oh."*

If there were any doubts about whether she'd heard my name before, they were confirmed.

"Captain Allen," I said. I held up the piece of yellow paper. "Is this not a legitimate invitation for the community to get involved and help you with a current case?"

Tex's eyes shifted from my face to the flyer and back to my face. He raised his eyebrows but didn't make a move otherwise.

"I'm a member of the community, and as you know, I have experience with this sort of thing. You may also remember that I have a fair amount of free time on my hands thanks to a certain situation regarding my business."

"Let's talk in my office." Tex turned and walked down the hall.

Imogene picked up a notepad and pen and followed him.

I put my hand on her arm. "I think he means me."

"Oh," she said for the third time. Her face fell as the opportunity for potential research slipped out of her grasp. "Okay." She set the notepad down and went back to the printer.

"This isn't a good idea," Tex said once we reached his office. He closed the door behind me, and I unclipped Rocky's leash and let him sniff the room. It wasn't his first trip to the police station, and he likely recognized Wojo's—or another dog's—scent.

"Hear me out," I said. "I have free time. I can help you. Brandon's waiting for me to trip up. I can't sit around and do nothing." I was ashamed of my desperation and neediness, and the recent memory of volunteering my time at the funeral home didn't help. If Tex suspected I was wrestling with inner demons, he didn't mention it.

"Did something happen this morning?"

"The reporter at my house," I said. "I think I should talk to them. They're not going to leave me alone until I do."

"Your call," he said. "I've been on both sides of a thing like this. No matter what you tell them, you can't control how the press is going to make you look."

"I know." I leaned back and stared at his desk. "I need a distraction. Right now, there's no place for me to go. I don't want to sit alone in Thelma Johnson's house pretending I'm not there so they'll go away."

He leaned back and stared at me. I held his gaze. We both knew what I was thinking.

"What do you have in mind?"

"If Brandon catches me doing anything decorating-related, he's going to use it against me. Your volunteer watch group is open to the public. It's a diversion."

"This case is going to take up most of my free time."

I held up my hands. "I'm not asking for you to entertain me. I knew exactly what I was getting into—what we were getting into —when we started this."

A slight grin curled Tex's mouth. "This."

"Yes. This." I paused a moment and allowed a smile of my own. I reached across the desk and touched his hand, and a spark of electricity shocked me. I pulled away, but he was quicker, grabbing my fingers and holding them in his own. His nails were clipped down to the quick, and his fingers were warm.

"This isn't me inserting myself in one of your cases," I said in a soft voice. "It's me needing to do something that isn't my job. You know I'm good at this. And like it or not, I'm already involved."

Tex leaned back in his chair. The seat tilted, and the springs creaked. He ran his open hand over his hair and then leaned forward and propped his elbows on the desk.

"That's all true. Everything you said is true. I can trust you to not talk to the press, and I know you'll tell me anything that seems odd. Your BS meter is well refined."

"Except when it came to you," I said.

He grinned, but the smile faded quickly. "Night, this case is going to get a lot of attention. The public is down on cops, and we're understaffed. I'm still waiting on a full report from Lloyd, but when the press finds out those bodies weren't discovered for days, they'll give the public more reason to call us ineffective."

"That's why you should take my offer of help. Your new desk manager – nice woman, by the way – has a stack of about two hundred of these out there." I tapped the yellow paper. "This call for volunteers was already in motion before I stepped foot inside your doors."

"No, Night. Not this time."

"I don't get it. You're looking for help canvassing the area, and you know you can trust me. What am I missing?"

"Leave it alone." He sneezed.

"Do you have a cold?" I asked.

"Allergies," he said. "Caffeine helps. Not many people know that." He gulped down the contents and set it on his desk. "Imogene?" he called toward the door. "I need more coffee."

"I'm on it," Imogene called back from the front. The next thing I heard was the sound of running water.

Tex kept talking. "The hikers who found the second body went to the press. They claim we're withholding information that could put more residents at risk."

I pointed over my shoulder. "Is that why you have a citizen at the desk instead of an officer?"

"Garcia took a sick day."

"Allergies too?"

"No. His wife's been threatening to leave him, and looks like she did it this time. He hasn't heard from her in days. He's got two kids in grade school, and his police officer salary doesn't pay enough for him to hire a sitter."

"Where did you find Imogene?"

"She found us. Applied over the internet and then followed up with phone calls and a face-to-face. I wish my officers were as tenacious as she was."

"She wants something," I said. "When people are properly motivated, they show a singlemindedness in getting what they want."

Tex sat back in his chair, and Rocky hopped up onto his lap. Tex ran his hands over Rocky's fur and then bent down and appeared to sniff him. He lifted one of Rocky's paws and studied the pads then lowered the paw and looked at me. "Like you?"

I sensed I was stepping into a trap, but Tex already knew I could be focused when necessary. "Sure. You've seen me go after things I want."

"What did you want from White Rock Lake this morning?"

There were times when dating a cop had distinct disadvantages, and this was one.

"Nothing. I wanted a place to go. I can't go to my studio or to a job site. I can't pick out paint samples or make an appointment with an estate sale or visit with a client. Yesterday, the park was one of my favorite spots in the city, and today it's the drop site for two bodies."

"Were you going to tell me?"

"I thought if you didn't want people there, you'd have it restricted. There were no cops, no reporters, and no police tape. I didn't think it mattered."

"There's a difference between me officially keeping the public out and me not wanting you to spend time at a site where two bodies were found. You get that, don't you?"

"It was broad daylight."

"Not the point."

I wasn't going to insert some clichéd "you can't tell me what to do" into our conversation. Tex didn't have issues with equality or empowerment, and he knew I could think for myself. But the lack of evidence surrounding this case had him at a standstill, and knowing the killer of a diabolical crime was out there made him think about things differently.

"Your powers of deduction are impressive," I said. "Did you know I was at the park based on the scent on Rocky's paws?"

"No. I saw you on the security feed from the camera my team installed this morning."

15

"ALL THIS TIME YOU KNEW I WAS THERE? YOU SAW ME ON CAMERA?"
I asked.

Tex nodded. "Good thing, too. I might never have known about the break in the fence if this little guy hadn't run underneath it." He rubbed the fur on top of Rocky's head. "Good boy."

"You saw that?"

"I did. I saw him charge toward the mortuary, and I called Arnold and let him know he was about to have a visitor. Nice driving, by the way."

Ooooooh!

I stood up and reached for Rocky's collar. He turned around on Tex's lap and looked at me as if to say, "Not yet."

"How do you know Arnold Akins?" I asked.

"I met him at a fundraiser. We have mutual supporters. Nice guy. A little creepy. A man who makes a living off death—I imagine that career path doesn't appeal to most people."

"I find the business of death to be somewhat comforting.

People die, but life doesn't stop." I was silent for a moment before continuing. "But then, some people may think I'm creepy."

His eyes moved from my face to my head. "You're an independent businesswoman who wears hats that look like flowerpots."

"I didn't say you thought I was creepy, but then again, you're a homicide detective. There's a sliding scale of normal when it comes to you and me."

"You spent a long time inside. Waiting out the rain?"

"I talked to Arnold, the owner's son, and then Edward, the father. Arnold told me about their financial problems."

"That's sort of private for a business, don't you think?"

"What can I say? People like to talk to me."

"What did he tell you?"

"The city wants to buy the mortuary and expand the public park. Edward borrowed money from Winston Burr, but when he defaulted on the loan payments, the deed went into Winston's hands. Arnold doesn't know if Winston is going to keep them on in salaried positions or sell the place to the city. Winston is one of your biggest donors too, isn't he? Is that how you met Arnold?"

"Something like that." Tex leaned back and held an unsharpened Dixon Ticonderoga pencil in front of Rocky, who nibbled at the yellow wood like it was an ear of corn. "Walk me through your morning."

"I went to the pool, and Nasty showed up. She's helping me with the lawsuit. Before she left the locker room, she picked up a blue rose petal like the one we found at the park. I didn't realize it at the time, but I must have tracked it home with me. I went home and checked the soles of my boots and found a ribbon with faded gold lettering."

"Where's this ribbon now?"

I pulled the envelope out of my bag and handed it to Tex. "I showed it to George to find out how common cream ribbon was. I didn't use an evidence bag because I didn't want to freak her out. She said the ribbon was a standard supply for a florist. Even though the letters are faded, she immediately knew it said, 'Rest in Peace.' The blue rose petal was the opposite. She said most florists steer clear of modified colors. That's where I ran into Brandon."

"Unbelievable," Tex said. "I have a team of officers in the field, and they still haven't connected those dots."

"When I left By George, I drove to the pavilion. All I was trying to do was to stay away from home. Rocky ran through the fence, and I went after him."

I sensed Tex's frustration. His investigations usually started with the discovery of a body, which led to the victim's identity, which led to the process of determining the victim's last twenty-four hours and the major players in a case. As far as I knew, this was the first time the discovery of the bodies led to a dead end. Under normal circumstances, Tex would know who the victims were. He'd have contacted the families and assigned a team of investigators to assemble the story of their murder. The longer things went before he had those breadcrumbs to follow, the colder the trail would become.

This lack of evidence left him in a bad place. The way the bodies had been discarded said something, but without any other concrete evidence, I didn't know what.

"Did you find anything from the flower shop?" I asked.

"No evidence of foul play other than the blood and heel marks. I bagged what we found and turned it over to the lab. Lloyd's overworked and understaffed. Even with this being the top priority, it's going to take some time."

"Do you have any other leads?"

He shook his head. "That's what I'm hoping to get from the volunteers. Maybe somebody saw something. Fresh eyes might turn up something new."

"You don't expect to find a lead at the park," I guessed.

"What's your point?"

"I know you. After we found a second body, you spent the night going over those woods with a fine-tooth comb. You probably took leaf and soil samples. If there were something out there that could give you a direction, you would have found it. You don't believe for a second there are clues out there that you didn't find."

"A volunteer watch group mobilizes the public and gets them involved. When people feel like they're helping, they tend to criticize less. This might buy us time with the media." Tex sneezed again. He grabbed a tissue from a box on the side of his desk and blew his nose.

"What about the hikers who found the first body? Didn't one of them say he parked at the flower shop?"

"Everything they told us checks out. Unless I find out they're related to one of the victims, they're going in the file as good Samaritans who cooperated fully."

"Anybody else?"

"We talked to a string of businesses out that way who all saw a blue van with a white logo on the side. Nobody remembers what the business was, but the fact that it was unfamiliar might be all we need."

I sat up straighter. "There was an appliance repair van at Akins Funeral Home," I said. "Blue with a white logo."

"It could have been the same van."

"His name is Quinn. If you call Arnold, he can give you the guy's contact information."

Tex's cell rang. He held his finger up to his lips. "Allen," he answered. He pointed to Rocky, and I leaned over the desk and lifted the furry monster. "You got something?" He pulled a lined notepad toward him and jotted notes while he listened.

I clipped Rocky's leash onto his collar and stood to leave. Tex indicated for me to wait. I sat back down and stroked Rocky's fur while Tex finished his call.

"Thanks, Lloyd." He tossed his phone onto his desk and leaned back. He stared at the ceiling for a moment and then picked up his pen and chucked it across his desk.

"Bad news?" I asked.

He looked at me but didn't speak. I waited. I knew him well enough to know he'd tell me—or not tell me—whatever he'd learned when he was ready. I felt his internal conflict and watched it play across his face. Tex was good at hiding his thoughts behind an emotionless mask, but this time, his clear blue eyes showed concern.

Finally, he spoke. "Lloyd used a digital enhancement program to simulate the victims' faces and ran the results through recognition software. He thinks he has a match on the man. I've got to contact the wife and see if I can get a positive identity."

There was something else, something he wasn't saying. "You're concerned," I said.

"If Lloyd is right, then this one's going to get messy. The simulation software matched the victim to Winston Burr."

16

Even if I hadn't heard the name several times since this morning, I understood what this meant for Tex. Forget the local media. The murder of a high-profile city benefactor would make national news. The scrutiny of Tex and his department would be powerful, and any mistakes would be magnified. Winston Burr had been the biggest public supporter of the police department, and that complicated things further. The media would question the focus of the investigation, and their interference might get in the way of answers.

"What about the female victim?" I asked.

"No match with the system. Lloyd's still working on it, but so far she's not telling her story." His clear blue eyes held my own, and not for the first time I felt as if Tex could see my thoughts. "You have plans for the rest of the day?"

I shook my head.

He stood. "Come with me. This requires a woman's touch."

ROCKY WAS a frequent guest of the Lakewood Police Department, and Imogene agreed to watch him while Tex and I headed out on our field trip. I left my car at the police station and rode with Tex. I didn't mind the silence. Riding in a Jeep with the top down presents certain challenges when it comes to conversation, and I had a feeling Tex wasn't worried about small talk.

We drove across town, past the pocket of mid-century modern ranches where my clients generally lived, to an affluent neighborhood with meticulously tended lawns and garden beds. Public stretches of the median were covered with vivid florals in white, pink, and yellow, a vibrant contrast to the wild bluebonnets that grew throughout the rest of the city. I'd always found bluebonnets to be one of the prettier elements of Dallas, but it didn't surprise me that the common plant was nowhere to be seen in this private community.

We reached the end of a drive, flanked by concrete posts that supported statues of lions on either side of the gate. The gate opened, and Tex drove inside. He parked by a flight of stairs thirty feet from the front door. Whoever lived here didn't make it easy for people to sneak up on them.

"This is the Burr residence," I said. I leaned forward and studied the façade of the Renaissance-style house. It was perfectly symmetrical and bigger than four of my apartment buildings put together. I'd read a profile of the house in a local design journal and knew it was over fifteen thousand square feet inside. The grounds held a stone bridge, a duck pond, a putting green, and a pool.

"Yes," Tex said. "This is the Burr residence."

"The gates opened for you."

"They know my Jeep. I've been here before."

Tex didn't seem interested in fielding questions. I sat quietly and wondered why I was being invited along to this house, for this reason, on this day. We'd entered new territory, me and Tex, but he didn't cross boundaries without careful consideration. This had nothing to do with the shift in our personal relationship.

Tex parked his Jeep, and I walked with him to the front door. He rang the bell, and chimes inside announced us. The door opened, and an attractive redhead in a cobalt-blue cashmere T-shirt and white trousers answered the door. "Captain Allen," she said. "This is a surprise. Come on in." She smiled broadly and held the door open.

"Hello, Shira," Tex said. He turned to me. "Shira Burr, this is Madison Night."

The woman turned her smile toward me. "Nice to meet you, Madison. I read about you, didn't I? You're the decorator with the Doris Day touch."

"That's me," I said, somewhat surprised to be known by someone like her.

"Don't worry about that article," she said with a comforting smile. "Those reporters are just trying to sell papers."

"That's what he said," I replied, glancing toward Tex.

I peered down the hallway at the expanse of the living room, easily twenty feet deep. An entire ranch house would fit on her first floor!

Shira shut the door behind us and addressed Tex. "Captain Allen, I hope you didn't come out here to talk to Winnie," she said. "He's been out of town on business for a few days. I expected him back this morning, but he must have extended his trip. Would you like a drink?"

"Iced tea would be great," Tex said.

We followed Shira through the foyer to a sitting room. Aside from an empty vase on the coffee table, the room appeared ready for company. A bar cart held a pitcher of fresh iced tea. Shira added a few ice cubes to two glasses and then filled them, handing one to each of us. It seemed like the most normal thing in the world to her, having a pitcher of tea sitting out for unexpected guests. I carried my tea to the loveseat but remained standing. Tex didn't move from the bar cart.

"When did Winston leave?" he asked.

"Last week. Tuesday, I think it was."

"Have you talked to him since he left?"

"Winnie and I have been married for thirty-three years. When he travels on business, it's best that he doesn't worry about me." She smiled. "I think he knows I secretly enjoy having the place to myself every now and then. A chance to go out with the girls or stay in and read."

"So you haven't heard from your husband since last Tuesday."

Shira's face paled, and her eyes moved across Tex, cut to me, and then back to Tex. "Captain Allen, this is starting to feel like something other than a social visit. Why are you here?"

I noticed the glass of tea in Tex's hand. He hadn't raised it to his lips, and cold condensation collected on the outside in beads. It was a prop. It was a thing to hold while he asked questions before delivering the news he'd come here to share.

"Shira, I came here as a friend. Two bodies were found by White Rock Lake late last night. We don't know how long they've been there. I have reason to believe one of those victims is your husband."

Whatever color was left in Shira's face drained. She reached out and clutched the arm of the bar cart for stability but didn't collapse. She turned away from us and poured two inches of scotch into a crystal tumbler then downed it in one big gulp. She set the glass on the cart and put both hands on the edge. Her back was to us, and I imagined her struggling to get her emotions under control. In one quick gesture, she picked up the decanter of scotch and flung it at the fireplace, where it smashed against the slate and spewed amber liquid across the floor.

She turned to face Tex. Her eyes were bloodshot, though no tears ran down her face. "I'll get my bag." I saw her chest heave and fall, and then she strode out of the room.

I GRABBED TEX'S ARM. "I SHOULDN'T BE HERE FOR THIS," I whispered.

"Not now, Night." He moved my hand off his arm but squeezed my fingers before letting go.

Shira Burr returned to the foyer with a platinum quilted handbag in her hand. She put on a pair of tortoiseshell sunglasses and closed the bag. She kept it in her hand like a clutch with the chain dangling by her leg. "I'm ready," she said.

The three of us left. I tried to picture Shira wedged between Tex and me in the Jeep, but a shiny black sedan sat in the carport. "Madison, go with Shira," Tex said.

I agreed. It was clear my presence on this trip wasn't incidental, though I remained in the dark. I followed Shira to the car and eased into the passenger side while she got behind the wheel.

We drove in silence. At one point, Shira reached across the center console and took my hand. Her grip was tight as if she were searching for something to stabilize her while the possibility of what she was about to discover spun her out of control. I squeezed back and hoped the gesture took the place of all the thoughts I didn't know how to verbalize.

We drove south, past the children's hospital, to the Dallas County Medical Examiner and Coroner's Office. The flat-roofed building took up a city block. We parked by the front doors, and I helped Shira out of the car and kept my arm around her as Tex exited the Jeep. I watched the reflection of the three of us as we approached the glass doors. Shira's bright-blue sweater and white pants seemed unnaturally festive, as did my blue-and-white suit and flowerpot hat. Only Tex, in his polo shirt and jeans, seemed dressed for the occasion.

Inside the Medical Examiner's office, a lanky white man with a freshly shaven head and a neatly trimmed goatee greeted Tex. "Captain Allen," he said. If we weren't in a medical examiner's office, I would have guessed him to be in the fashion industry. His hip Fred Perry polo shirt was buttoned up to the top button and paired with jeans made from Japanese denim. The jeans narrowed at the ankle and revealed plaid socks and tennis sneakers. The one clue to his real profession was the white lab coat that hung from the back of his chair.

"Lloyd, this is Mrs. Burr and Ms. Night." Tex nodded his head toward each of us in turn. "Ladies, this is Lloyd."

Lloyd held out his hand, and I shook it. He moved on to Shira, who kept her dark glasses on and focused on a spot on the desk. When it seemed obvious she wasn't interested in a handshake, he dropped his arm to his side. "Can I get anyone anything? Water? Coffee? Tea?"

"Let's not pretend this is a social call," Shira said. She tipped her head back and shook it, and her long red tresses fell from her shoulder and hung down her back. She kept the sunglasses on and hooked her hand in the crook of Tex's arm.

"Of course," Lloyd said. He led us down a narrow hallway.

I'd never been asked to identify a body and wasn't sure why I was being given access to the process now, but being naturally inquisitive, I followed along. My gut was clenched in anticipation of seeing a body in a state of decay, and the cheese danish in my stomach turned.

Lloyd reached a room and opened the door. I expected an exposed concrete floor and a row of metal cabinets with sleek aluminum handles. Instead, we entered a comfortable sitting room filled with tufted chairs positioned around a round wood table made of maple. Soft music, so quiet it was almost unnoticeable, created a soothing backdrop. The walls were devoid of art, and a potted plant sat in the corner.

"Please take a seat, Mrs. Burr," Lloyd said.

Shira dropped into a chair, and Tex sat to her left. He pointed to the chair to her right, and I took that. Lloyd sat opposite her. He placed a black folder on the table and flipped it open, looked at Tex, and nodded.

"Shira, I know this is hard," Tex said. "Lloyd is going to show you some pictures. They're identifying characteristics from the body we found by White Rock Lake. I need you to tell me whether you think this is Winston."

"Have you seen the pictures?" she asked.

"Yes."

"But you still need me to see them?"

"Yes."

She turned to Lloyd and held out her hand. He handed her a photo face down, and she flipped it over. Almost instantly, she placed the photo face down again and pushed it back toward Lloyd. "It's him," she said.

She started to stand, and Tex put his hand on her arm. "There's a second victim. She seems to have suffered the same fate as your husband. Lloyd ran the same simulation program to give us an idea of what she might have looked like when she was alive. You know Winston's contacts better than anyone. Would you be willing to look at a separate set of photos to help us out?"

She nodded. Lloyd pulled a second photo out of the stack and pushed it toward Shira. She flipped it over and stared at it. Unlike with her husband, this time she had no noticeable reaction.

"Do you recognize her?" Tex prompted.

Shira set the photo face up on the table.

"No," she said. "If I've met her, I don't remember. I'm sorry, Captain. I meet a lot of people every day. I know you were hoping for a different answer, but I'm afraid I can't help you out."

WE FINISHED up with Lloyd and left. Shira insisted she was okay to drive, though Tex and I followed her sedan from a few car lengths back to make sure she made it home safely. When she pulled past the gates, Tex drove forward and turned around at the end of the road.

"Explain my role in what we did," I said.

"I needed a female witness." He turned the wheel and swerved around an errant skateboard. "I told you this case is going to be messy. Winston and Shira Burr are a big deal in this town. They're also the biggest donors to the annual police budget. People are going to watch this investigation closely."

"You've conducted cases under public scrutiny before. Why does the idea of close attention bother you now?"

"Winston's support of the force isn't a secret, but there are two victims here, and the longer we go before we know who the woman is, the more it's going to look like we don't care about her."

"You think people are going to turn this into a rich people vs. poor people thing," I guessed.

"I wouldn't blame them. Half of this town is swimming in wealth, and the other half pretends to be. Now you get a case of two people with no apparent connection being the victims of a double homicide. Winston's wealth is going to put the focus of the investigation on him, but I don't know if this was about him or her. I don't know who she was to him. Without more information, I can't caution the residents about how to stay safe."

Tex pulled out of the gates of the private community where the Burr residents lived and onto a heavily trafficked street. It was rush hour, and no matter what roads you chose, you got caught in a glut of people making their way home at the end of their day. We sat at a red light behind a long chain of cars.

"People are going to say we were in his pocket," he said.

The light changed, and the cars ahead of us inched forward.

"A lot of this city was in his pocket. From what I've heard, Winston Burr was a philanthropist."

"No, Winston Burr was a successful businessman who understood that money bought him power. He's made a lot of enemies through his developments and negotiations, but he spread his wealth around to offset that hostility."

"Did you like him?"

He looked at me.

"Were you friends?"

"We were acquaintances. I enjoyed his scotch, his poker game, and, on occasion, his membership to the country club."

"What about Shira?"

"Shira Burr was devoted to her husband and him to her. They had one of those public marriages that makes you think some people get to have it all."

As Tex got onto the highway, my phone lit up with an incoming call from Bianca's Restaurant. It was a Salvadorian spot across the street from Mad for Mod that I often frequented for lunch. It was run by a dark-haired Latina woman named Bianca. With me staying away from my place of work, I'd also stayed away from my usual haunts. It didn't seem possible that my repeat business would make a difference to their bottom line, but I couldn't imagine another reason for Bianca to call me.

"This is Madison," I answered.

"Thank god. You're okay?" Bianca's voice was recognizable, though tinged with urgency.

"Yes, I'm okay. I'm sorry I haven't been in for a while. Mad for Mod is closed, but it's temporary—"

She cut me off. "You're not in your shop? You don't know?"

"Know what?"

"You better drop everything and get over here. Somebody vandalized your showroom."

18

"Vandals?" I repeated. "Did you see who did it? Did you see what they took?"

"I was busy with the restaurant. I'm sorry, Madison, I wish I could tell you more."

Tex took the next exit and doubled back the way we'd come.

"I'm on my way." I hung up.

I relayed the details while Tex drove. "You don't think this has to do with the lawsuit, do you?" I asked.

"Brandon would have to be pretty stupid to do something like this."

"Why would someone loot a mid-century modern decorator showroom? What did they think they would get? A tiki bar?"

"What was inside your front window?"

"An outdoor picnic scene. I used an old grill with a simulated flame, a basket like the one we had at the park, and a checkered blanket."

I didn't want to think about the damage to the massive front window or what might have been stolen, but either way, I was looking at a major expense. Furniture might have been prohibitive to looters, but there were enough smaller items used to accessorize my display space to be easy pickings.

It was equally possible that the looters, not finding anything of value to steal, had vandalized the place out of anger. Beyond the picnic scene inside the window was a Group S420 silver-finished ball-and-rod-framed modular seating arrangement with original blue Unika Vaev upholstery, and a small collection of Danish modern tables. If vandals damaged either one, I'd be out thousands in inventory and future profits.

Tex couldn't drive fast enough. My heart was in my throat as we turned the corner onto Greenville Avenue. Two fire trucks were parked willy-nilly in the street in front of Mad for Mod. Tex swung the Jeep into Bianca's parking lot, and I was out before the brake was on.

A small cluster of people stood in the corner of Bianca's lot, making no secret of their interest in the activities. I counted three with their cell phones up, recording the action.

I ignored the crowd and ran to Bianca, a stout woman with dyed black hair, talking to one of the firemen. He held his hand palm-side out. "I'm sorry, ma'am, this area is off-limits."

"I'm the owner," I said. I turned to Bianca. "Thank you for calling me."

"I'm so sorry, Madison." Bianca squeezed my hand. "I have to get back inside." She excused herself and crossed the street and went into her restaurant.

"You're Madison Night?" the fireman asked.

"Yes," I said, a little out of breath from running across the street. I put my hands on my waist to stave off a side stitch. "What happened? Was there a fire?"

He pointed to a small, overturned grill that I'd used as a prop.

Inside the grill was an electric lamp that was designed to look like a campfire. I'd picked it up on clearance from a Halloween store a few years ago. I'd thought it added a note of realism to the display. "The restaurant owner thought that was a live flame." He looked over my head and adjusted his helmet. "Captain Allen," he said.

Tex peered into the broken glass. After a long stretch, he dropped his hands and turned to face us. "Hannigan," he said with a nod of recognition. "I'm here unofficially. Ms. Night is a friend."

The fireman, Hannigan, looked back and forth between me and Tex. When he seemed to reach whatever conclusion he needed, he nodded. "Looks like routine vandalism. We see this from time to time."

Tex put his hands in the pockets of his jeans and stared at the damaged storefront. "And unofficially?"

Hannigan didn't say anything at first. I felt the tension between the two men: one in charge of this situation and the other in charge of keeping the city safe. One a stranger and one an intimate part of my life.

When Hannigan spoke, it wasn't what I expected. He turned to me. "Ms. Night, is there a reason you weren't at your business during regular hours?"

"I'm involved in a legal matter, and until it's settled, my business is closed."

"I imagine you're losing money every day that your business is closed?"

"I'm certainly not making any."

"Captain Allen, can I speak to you privately?" Hannigan asked.

I shifted my hands from my waist to my hips. "If this is about my business, then I think I should get to hear what you have to say."

"She's right," Tex said.

Hannigan didn't seem happy. "Unofficially, we don't see a lot of vandalism on Greenville Avenue. A brick through a window usually means looting." He looked at me. "Ms. Night, frankly, this looks like something a business owner might do if she wanted to collect insurance money."

"I resent that," I exclaimed.

"I'm sure you do, but if the police captain hadn't introduced you as a personal friend, I'm not sure I'd believe otherwise. This could be random, but it also very well could not. You might want to make a list of anybody who has a beef against you before the insurance company comes knocking on your door."

"What are you implying?"

"I might not doubt your story, but they sure will."

THERE WASN'T a lot I could do to secure the showroom, but I wasn't about to leave with a gaping hole in the front. Tex carried a sheet of particle board from behind the studio and positioned it inside. As we angled it into place, his phone rang. It was Lloyd. To Tex's credit, he seemed conflicted about leaving me.

"Go," I said. "You've been waiting for this call. I'll catch an Uber."

Tex got about three steps away when he turned back. "I don't want you to take an Uber."

"Why not? You do."

"Night, I'm serious. Call a friend or wait here until I come back. This isn't the time to start trusting strangers."

I went inside Mad for Mod, scanned the broken glass on the floor and the damage to the Unika Vaev upholstery, and called the one person who would offer me something other than consolation.

"What?" Nasty said in lieu of hello.

"Someone vandalized my showroom."

"Where are you now?"

"Where do you think? There's a hole in my front window. I'll be here for the rest of the day, packing up files and moving furniture to the storage locker out back."

"No, you won't. Get out of there, Madison."

"I know you don't respect my aesthetic, but this is what I do. I can't leave it for people to destroy."

"I'll send Gerry's team in to take possession of your inventory."

"I'm not going to give Gerry Rose my inventory."

Nasty's voice was flat and unemotional, a counterpoint to my rising hysteria. "Madison, this sounds like a trap. The vandalism accomplished one thing: it got you to the place you shouldn't be. If Brandon's team gets evidence that you're doing anything remotely involving your job, it's going to be a lot harder to prove you're following the injunction."

19

I PICTURED THE CROWD ACROSS THE STREET, ARMED WITH CELL phone cameras and not afraid to use them. It wouldn't be difficult to prove I was at Mad for Mod, or that I'd spent hours inside the store after the firemen left. But regardless of Nasty's words of caution, I couldn't leave. Too much was at stake, including confidential client files. It was one thing to put my livelihood at risk, but another to allow sensitive information to be stolen. I could win a bogus lawsuit, I believed, but I'd never recover from a data breach.

From the moment I looped Nasty in, I'd followed her advice. It wasn't that I believed her to have some insight I didn't, but there comes a point at which you question whether your instincts are serving you. For me, that point came around the same time the legal papers were served.

Last October, I won a local design competition, and winning brought opportunity. Between that and an abandoned pajama factory that I inherited and converted into a shared workspace, businesses in Dallas took notice of my work. It didn't hurt that my quirky mid-century designs were appealing to a demographic who grew up on a diet of Tim Burton movies and Snapchat filters. My inspiration might have been the sets of the Doris Day movies I studied, but the end result was unique to an audience who never heard of *Pillow Talk*, and in a world mostly designed by their parents' parents, "unique" held value.

Through my time in Dallas, I watched historical societies try to educate residents about the legacy of an architect. I saw once-gorgeous buildings fall into disarray after being granted historical significance because tenants chose not to keep up with the rigid expectations that came along with such designation.

I fully appreciated the beauty of the mid-century architecture around me, but I allowed for two potential client types: those who loved what I did and wanted to know everything about everything, and those who simply liked flat roofs and geometric shapes. Ikea had done us all a favor by making modern design attainable. I used to tell clients they could go the direction of reproductions and knockoffs and that would be fine, but I could decorate for them using original pieces I'd accumulated in my inventory. Initially, that pitch brought me loyal business. Lately, it was the most cited reason for clients choosing another firm over me.

That was why the lawsuit was so ironic. Brandon's designs were instantly recognizable thanks to the wholesale decorator discounts he received at reproduction houses around the country. I was as much a fan of the Barcelona chair as anybody, but when I incorporated the classic quilted leather and chrome piece into a design, it was an original that showed signs of a former life. I loved the nod to history, the evidence that this particular chair had existed through decades of change and generations of families. When requested, I had cushions reupholstered; there's not much you can do about claw holes in leather.

Conversely, Brandon ordered direct from companies who knocked off classic designs. It was style for profit's sake. I could respect the companies who reinvigorated the legacy of the design firms that started the mid-mod movement in the atomic era by producing classics according to original design specs, but I drew the line at copycats.

It was a good thing I'd left Rocky at the police station. Broken glass covered the interior carpet, and the risk to his paws would have been great. I went out back and dug past a pile of colorful PVC planter bowls and extracted a ShopVac I'd purchased at the local hardware store, then carried it inside and set to work vacuuming. With the help of several arc lamps aimed over the stretch of carpet in question, I was able to identify the scattered shards and focus my attention on removing them. Rocky wasn't my singular concern. Effie, my lone employee, occasionally kicked off her shoes and walked around the showroom barefoot between appointments, and the last thing I needed was to add workman's compensation to the challenges I juggled.

Brandon's lawsuit hurt Effie as well as me. She'd been saving for a vacation when I'd suspended business. Tex's maggots and subsequent dead bodies had distracted me from keeping in touch. It occurred to me that while I hadn't called her, she hadn't called me either.

I turned off the ShopVac and went into my office. Client files had been pulled out of the drawers and left scattered across the surface of my desk. One folder was open, and pages had fallen onto the floor. The corner of a prospective client profile lay in Rocky's water bowl. The corner was soaked through, and the ink bled over the page.

Mad for Mod had been closed for weeks. Any water that had been left in Rocky's bowl would have evaporated by now. Someone had been in here recently, and if it weren't me, it most likely would have been Effie.

A yellow 1970s donut phone sat on the corner of my one-of-a-kind desk. Despite the rest of the world embracing the convenience of speakerphones and Bluetooth devices, I loved conducting business on this one. I held the receiver and pressed the buttons of Effie's number by memory. After four rings, her voicemail answered.

"*¡Hola!* You've reached Effie. I'm in Meh-hee-co! I didn't spring for the international plan, so you better leave a message!" The phone beeped, and a second, robotic male voice continued. "The mailbox is full." The call disconnected.

I questioned the decision of telling anyone who called her that she was out of the country, but Effie was active on social media. No doubt the world already knew she was in Mexico. This message would come as no surprise.

Effie often joked about my penchant for donut phones and lack of interest in technology. She took the day off the last few times Apple released a new iPhone, switched to Galaxy products temporarily, and then returned to the Apple family when the supreme court reopened their case against Samsung. (Effie had been studying patent law at the time.) She didn't understand why anyone wouldn't have unlimited data, and she swore her phone was her life. How her voicemail could be full was beyond me—but I knew I'd tease her about it the next time we spoke.

I bent down to retrieve the now-wet sheet of paper and laid it on the copier. I started the machine and watched the duplicate spit out—smudged and blurry, but legible. It was when I picked up the copy that I discovered the file in question was that of By George.

Those files weren't supposed to be here. They'd been requested by Brandon's legal team, and I'd made a copy that I turned over to Nasty. She would have known better than to return them here. So where had these come from?

I corralled the rest of the fallen papers into one pile, and then, seeing I was alone with no chance of being interrupted by a client or a dog, dropped onto my butt and stretched my legs out in front of me. I sorted through the papers and put them back in order while decorating and legal conspiracies floated through my mind. All thoughts of Tex's case were replaced by my doubts about the future of Mad for Mod.

A key slipped into the lock of the back door, and before I could get in a position to defend myself, the door swung open. Considering all the change I'd experienced in the past year, I shouldn't have been surprised by the person who entered.

"Hudson?" I asked.

2 0

Hudson was my former handyman, and he existed on a steady diet of wood pulp and punk rock. He was also my former lover. After our breakup he'd headed out west to pursue the opportunity of turning a part of his life into something Hollywood could exploit. The last time we'd spoken, Hollywood had taken extreme liberties with the supporting cast of Hudson's life, including me, and I'd turned my back on the business they call show and hoped for the best. It had been months since we spoke.

"Madison," Hudson said. His voice was deep and scratchy as if he'd spent the day in a smoke-filled club. He held out his hand. I grabbed it, used my other to leverage myself against the desk, and stood. My skirt had twisted on me, and I quickly adjusted the fabric. My hat was somewhere on the floor.

"What are you doing back in Dallas? I thought you moved to Los Angeles."

"I'm here for a few days. I came by to say hello, and the place was locked up." He shifted his gaze, and his black hair fell forward and shielded his forehead.

Hudson was the sort of guy who looked like trouble but was safer than a room filled with kittens. He favored long sideburns, black T-shirts, leather jackets, and faded Lee 101 Rider jeans. While his wardrobe was a cross between Marlon Brando and James Dean, his looks were between Johnny Cash and Elvis. We matched in a way that catalog models were cast, but like models who merely looked the part, we lacked the chemistry to fully ignite a relationship. I felt lucky that we'd remained friendly.

"When did you get in?"

"This morning," he said. "I went by your house first and then came here. I wanted to give you a heads up. The movie is happening. There's a second unit in town to get establishing shots and reference material. So far they haven't decided if they're filming here or on a Hollywood backlot, but they want to explore their options."

"Can't they find that out on the internet?"

"I've learned not to question the path to genius." He glanced around. "The place is dark. What's going on?"

I leaned back against the desk. "Someone threw a brick through the front window. It's temporarily covered with plywood, but not as secure as I'd like. I'm afraid to leave the place unattended overnight."

"You still have those breeze blocks out back?"

I nodded. "They're stacked next to the recycling."

"They'll hold the plywood in place," he said. He paused. "I can bring them in if you want."

"Tex is dealing with police business," I said. I offered it as the answer to an unasked question.

Hudson shrugged. "I figured something like that."

My breakup with Hudson was not unconnected to my relationship with Tex. The two men had a checkered past, and the last I'd heard, in that story of Hudson's life, Hollywood had turned the character of Tex into a woman. I wasn't sure how that would play out, but unless I chose to get more involved, that wasn't my problem.

"I'd love your help," I said. "It'll go twice as fast with two of us."

I led Hudson out back. In the past, he'd given me more than I could have asked for, and without his presence, I'd had to adapt to doing things for myself. I felt his absence more deeply than he could have known, but it was professionally, not romantically, and that kept me from accruing any karmic debts I couldn't pay off.

I slipped on a pair of heavy canvas work gloves and grabbed a couple of breeze blocks. Hudson picked up twice as many with his bare hands. Together we made trip after trip until a makeshift wall of decorative concrete blocks held the plywood in place inside the window.

"Are you going to tell me what's going on with you?" he asked when we finished.

"I told you. It was vandalism. This sort of thing happens from time to time."

"It happens to the stores that people want to loot."

"What's your point?"

"Madison, you had a picnic scene in the window and an arrangement of vintage appliances on display. I don't know a lot of people who go looting to pick out a fifties-era oven."

I tapped my palm against the shiny red appliance. "They don't make them like they used to."

"You're in trouble again," he said. "I saw the reporters at your house."

"It's not what you think."

As we finished stacking the breeze blocks, Bianca came to the front door. Her black hair was pinned up and, judging from the lack of flyaways, held in place with enough hairspray to beat humidity at its own game. She knocked on the glass, and I unlocked it.

"I thought you might be hungry," she said. She handed me a container. Before I opened it, I knew it was packed with my favorite Salvadorian shrimp and chicken salad. "On the house. Vandalism special."

I accepted the container. "Thank you." I felt Hudson's stare on me. "Bianca, you remember Hudson, right?"

"Of course," Bianca said. "Nice to see you again." She pointed to the takeout container. "There's enough there for two."

I turned to Hudson. "Can you take this to my office?" I asked. "I'll be back in a moment."

"Sure."

As soon as Hudson was out of earshot, I turned back to Bianca. "Nobody at your place saw anything?" I asked hopefully.

"We're short-staffed. Vandals could have carried out half of your showroom, and I wouldn't have seen it." She shook her head. "I told my husband you can't find good help these days."

"If you do remember something, let me know. The police think this was random, but I'm not sure."

"You think someone wanted to send you a message?"

I didn't want to tell Bianca my suspicions that Brandon was behind the vandalism. Whatever I'd done to incur the wrath of the vandal, the sad fact remained that Bianca owned the business directly across the street from me. If someone had made me a target, then the businesses around me were targets by default. I had friends on Greenville Ave, but those friendships would dry up once my presence affected their earnings. This wasn't the time to test the lengths to which relative strangers would go for me.

"I don't know what to think. Nothing like this has happened before."

"I'll talk to my staff." She fished a handful of salsa packets out of her apron and thrust them at me. "Take care, Madison."

"You too."

I watched Bianca cross the street before rejoining Hudson in my office. I was surprised to find him standing on the opposite side of my desk, running his hand over the wood grain. He'd been the one to build it, combining bits and pieces from furniture that had been beyond repair. It was a Frankendesk of sorts, but it suited me.

"I thought you might have traded up by now," he said.

"You know me better than that." I smiled. I slipped the pages from the Brandon Montgomery file into their folder and slid the folder into the desk drawer.

"Are you hungry?" I opened the container and waved it under Hudson's nose.

"Madison, your business is closed, you have reporters at your house, and your front window had a brick thrown through it. Are those things related?"

"They might be."

"How are they related to the case Tex is working on?"

I looked up from the salad to Hudson's face. "Tex's case? He has nothing to do with this. Why would you think that?"

"A lot of people don't like police. You've made no secret of your relationship with their captain. It's not a stretch to think this attack on you was a message to him."

UNTIL HUDSON OFFERED HIS THEORY, I'D BEEN DEAD SET ON Brandon Montgomery being behind the vandalism. Was it possible that my relationship with the police had brought on an unexpected level of violence?

"Nobody knows Tex and I are dating," I said. "We agreed to keep things quiet."

"You don't have to tell people you two are involved for them to connect you," Hudson said. "You've been on the fringes of five of Tex's cases, one of them so famous a couple of Hollywood producers bought the rights."

"Yes, but that's your story, not ours."

"They can't tell my story without mentioning you."

I blushed. When Hudson was first approached about the rights to his story, he'd checked with me first. The story in question regarded the now-famous Pillow Stalker of Dallas, and details of the case had pulled me, Hudson, and Tex into diametrically opposed angles. While we'd all been personally involved in varying ways, Hudson's story—living under false accusations, rumors, and gossip for nearly twenty years while building a life of his own—held the most interest to the husband-wife team who approached him.

As someone who preferred privacy to fame, Hudson had surprised me by pursuing the opportunity. I ultimately recognized that profiting from the story in the aftermath might be the only way for him to accept what he'd lost when living under a cloud of suspicion. We'd been romantically involved at the time, and I've found it's easier to accept differences of opinion from people you start to believe are "the one."

"Madison, I don't know when the last time was that you stopped to look at the world around you, but there's a growing anti-cop sentiment out there. I have a lot of reasons not to like the police, and that's not jealousy talking."

"Tex is a dedicated officer. He makes a difference."

"Yes, he does. And in a lot of ways, you're safer with him than you ever were with me."

I reached my hand out and put it on his forearm. "Hudson . . ."

He tapped the back of my hand. "Madison," he said and then continued in a softer voice. "In a lot of ways, you're safer with him, but in some ways, you're not. His enemies are your enemies. His battles are your battles. Once people connect you two, you won't be able to escape that."

If I'd had any doubts about Tex vs. Hudson, they cleared at that moment. Because when Hudson signed on as a consultant to the writing team penning the script of the Pillow Stalker, I wanted nothing to do with the process. Early attempts to reach me to fact-check and explore my emotional state for character development had gone unanswered and ignored. I wouldn't interfere with Hudson pursuing what he wanted, but I didn't want to be a part of it.

With Tex, I didn't think twice about being there to support him. I defended him without question, and I told whoever would listen that the local police were the good guys despite the growing anti-cop sentiment.

"Hudson, how much of our story are we going to see when this movie comes out?"

"That depends on what you tell them," he said. "They know my side of things, and they said they haven't been able to reach you."

"I didn't want to step on your experience," I said.

"You're as much a part of that story as I am. Maybe more. They're going to write it how they see it, and that includes your role."

"That doesn't bother you? That my point of view isn't about you?"

"I've got a piece of the profits," Hudson said with a wink. "The better the story, the better the box office."

I squeezed Hudson's hand. "Thank you for your help today. Now, if you'll excuse me, I have a couple of phone calls to make."

It would have been too easy to ask Hudson for a ride home. I walked him to the door and thanked him again then returned to my office. I ate a few bites of Bianca's salad, but despite how tasty it was, my appetite was nonexistent. I put the container in my minifridge and called the police station.

"Lakewood Police Department," said a now-familiar female voice.

"Imogene?" I asked. "This is Madison Night. Captain Allen's friend."

"Sure, I remember. He's on-site with the medical examiner. I'll tell him you called."

"Actually, I wanted to talk to you."

"Me? Okay," she said. Her voice faltered.

"What can you tell me about the community volunteer group you were organizing?"

She waited a beat, but I did not chime in to fill the silence. A moment later, she spoke. "The group is meeting tomorrow night in the community room of Alejandro's Restaurant. Captain Allen asked a member of the Dallas Police Department to run the meeting. We're all hoping Captain Allen gets something from Lloyd. Otherwise, there's not a lot to go on."

"Two unidentified bodies dropped at the perimeter of the White Rock Lake picnic area. Minimal evidence and crime scene ruined by weather conditions. You're right, it's not much."

"I know!" she exclaimed. "If I were writing this, I'd have clues all over the place by now." The phone made a beeping noise. "Can I put you on hold? There's a call coming in."

"I can—sure," I said. Imogene could ask Tex for my contact information, but until he and I had a sit-down, I wanted to keep this between us.

I moved from the edge of my desk to around back and sat in my chair. The memory foam felt comfortable under my near-numb butt cheek. As I listened to the background music, I pulled the By George file back out of my desk drawer and flipped it open. I was caught between Tex's trouble and my own, and Hudson's theory suggested they might be the same.

Hudson had been talking about the vandalism, but what if the same logic applied to the lawsuit? Was it possible Brandon Montgomery was so angry about the By George design job that he turned to violence? I grabbed a pen and made a note on the inside of the folder: *Brandon – vandalism?* Underneath I drew a daisy, not because it had anything to do with anything but because the extended amount of time on hold motivated me to doodle.

In the time it took me to draw a daisy, a leaf, some grass, and a shrub, Imogene returned to the phone. "Madison, are you still there?" she asked.

"Yes."

"That was Captain Allen. I told him you were on the line, and he gave me a message. Hold on, I want to get it right. He said, 'If you're calling for information about the case, no comment.' You're a decorator, aren't you? That's what he told me to say to the press."

"I suppose that means he doesn't have any new leads."

"None that he told me about."

I thanked Imogene and called Tex's cell. I wasn't looking to get information; I was looking to give it.

"Allen," Tex answered.

"It's me. Do you have a sec?"

"Didn't Imogene give you my message?"

"I didn't call you to talk about the case."

"Okay. What's up?"

I went with the rip-off-the-Band-Aid approach. "Hudson's in town," I said quickly.

"Yeah, I thought I saw his truck earlier today."

Not for the first time, I marveled at Tex's powers of observation and ability to compartmentalize information. "He came by my studio and offered a fresh theory on the vandalism."

"What's that?"

"He suggested it might have something to do with my relationship to the police." I wasn't sure if I needed to supply more details, so I paused and gauged the silence as best as I could. "If there's someone out there who doesn't like you—"

"It's possible," Tex said.

I'd been secretly hoping Tex would discount Hudson's opinion, but him agreeing without much thought gave the idea more validity, not less. "Do you think it could have something to do with your current case?"

"My gut says no. We're too early on in this investigation. Whoever did it is probably watching the news to see what we know, and until five minutes ago, we didn't know much. After the news tonight, maybe I could see it, but if someone's using you to send a message to me, it's based on general discontent, not anything specific."

"I suppose that makes sense," I said.

"I'm going to stick around work for a bit," Tex said. "It's close to ten. This might be another all-nighter."

"Where are the dogs?"

"They're playing in my office. I'll take them to my place so you can get a solid night of sleep."

I told Tex to call me when he was done. Having shut out most of the world and created a life with my dog, I wasn't a fan of letting Rocky sleep elsewhere. That's the beauty of being the parent to a fur baby. There's no resentment when you choose not to cut the apron strings.

I closed the By George file and called Nasty. Under any other circumstances I would have called a friend for a ride, but Nasty had become an unexpected confidante.

"Big Bro Security," Nasty answered.

"Donna, it's Madison. I'm still at my studio, and I was hoping we could meet to go over a few things."

"I thought I told you to get out of there."

"I need a ride. Plus there's something I think you should see."

"I'm in the area. Hold that thought."

A few minutes after hanging up, a silver Saab swung into my old parking space. Overhead lights mounted to the back of my building cast a yellow glow over the lot. A misty drizzle of rain was visible in the light.

Nasty got out of her car. She was wearing a white sleeveless tank top and denim-colored leggings with a stretchy panel to accommodate her pregnant belly. She hadn't yet traded her platform stilettos for sensible shoes, and at this point, I wondered if she ever would.

She tipped her head and pulled her cascade of hair over her left shoulder and then strode to the back of the showroom and let herself in. "What's up?"

I told her about the vandalism, the open file on the By George job, and Hudson's theory that the vandalism could be linked to the police and not the lawsuit. Nasty listened attentively and waited until I was finished to speak.

"He might be right. I want to talk more about this, but not tonight. I have another job." She checked her Rolex. "Tell me what you can on the drive to your place, and we'll pick back up tomorrow."

I grabbed my handbag and keys and followed her outside. "Shouldn't you be taking it easy or tasking out projects to that staff of yours?"

She glared at me. "I'm pregnant. I'm not dead." A beat passed between us. She put her hand on her belly and rubbed it in a circular motion. "Move it. I don't have time for your nonsense."

"Hormones?"

"No, that was me being me."

She let the car idle while I buckled the seatbelt and then

backed out of her space. She drove to the exit and waited while two cars drove past.

"I can't help you with the Brandon Montgomery thing anymore," she said. "The police have a new case that connects back to one of Gerry's friends, and as a personal favor, I'm keeping an eye on things. The media is trying to turn it into a class war. I need to spend my time on that."

"You're investigating the murders by White Rock Lake," I guessed.

"How do you know about the murders?" Nasty asked. She pulled out of the parking lot onto the street.

"I found one of the bodies."

She slammed on the brakes. Even though we'd been going less than five miles an hour, I lurched against the seatbelt. "Madison, I think we just figured out how you're going to pay me back."

2 2

"I'm not going to hinder a police investigation," I said. "You were a cop, Donna. I appreciate your help with my legal problems, but you can't expect me to risk my relationship with Tex for you."

"I'm not trying to break you two up. Tex talks to you. He trusts you."

"That's right. Because he knows I respect his job."

"Do we need to recap how many times your involvement in an investigation made his job more difficult?"

My righteous indignation faltered. "Point taken."

"Like I was saying, he'll talk to you. And he knows I'm helping you with the lawsuit, so he probably assumes you'll talk to me."

"Tex might talk to me, but not about his cases. And why do you care?"

Nasty drove around the block and pulled back into my parking lot. This time she put the car in park. "I've been wanting to expand Big Bro Security from businesses to private residences, and my plan was to land the Burrs as a client so the rest of the neighborhood would follow. The news says Winston Burr was

128

one of the victims found at the lake. Did you find him, or did you find Yasmine Garcia?"

I barely heard the second half of what she said. I felt the heat leave my body, and my mind populated with new questions.

"Yasmine Garcia is the second victim?" I choked out. "Officer Garcia's wife?" My flesh broke out in goosebumps, and my heartbeat picked up.

"Tex didn't tell you?" Nasty had the courtesy to look surprised.

Tex had an obligation to protect his case, but to get the news from Nasty and not him still stung. "He didn't say anything. I suppose he was trying to protect his officer."

"He better watch that. I have four witnesses who saw the Garcias arguing at a public restaurant on Greenville Avenue two weeks ago, and one says the argument devolved quickly. He accused her of cheating, and she said their marriage was a joke. I'm waiting on security footage from the restaurant to see if I can back up the gossip with evidence, but his wife turning up dead not long after a public argument puts him on the suspect list."

"Officer Garcia is a pussycat."

"He's a cop. You don't become a cop unless you've got a strong need to right wrongs and deliver justice. If he had a loose wire, then his idea of justice might veer into territory most people would avoid."

I watched Nasty's face as she talked. She'd been a cop, too. She claimed leaving the force and starting her company had more to do with leaving a toxic male workplace and wanting something for herself, but if what she'd said was true, then she had the same internal needs as Garcia and Tex. I wanted to believe the best about people, but I'd already seen too many examples of people who thought they were above the law.

Nasty put the car in drive and left my parking lot again. This time, she headed toward my house. As she drove, I thought about my conversation with Tex. He hadn't flinched when I mentioned Hudson's theory, which told me he didn't discount it. But the rest of the conversation left me wondering if he was protecting me or shutting me out.

"How much can I expect from Tex?" I asked.

My question could have been interpreted in two ways. I waited to see which way Nasty would go. She didn't take her eyes off the road. "Tex is under no obligation to share details of a case with you because you're sleeping with him."

"I told him a theory that's recently been floated to me, that maybe the vandalism had to do with him. He agreed it was a possibility. He was with Lloyd, the medical examiner, and he said he was hopeful."

"Cops don't use hope to solve cases. Not cops like Tex."

"I know."

"He knew about Yasmine Garcia when you talked, but he didn't want to tell you."

"That's what it sounds like."

"How'd you two leave things? Did you get mad and hang up on him?"

I balled my fists up in my lap. "Why do you assume I'm going to throw a temper tantrum when I don't get my way? I know there are parts of Tex's job that I am not privy to, and that me inserting myself in his investigations might unnecessarily complicate things both personally and professionally."

"But?"

I sighed. "But if the vandalism at my showroom has anything to do with the police, then things—both personal and professional —are complicated."

"Not necessarily."

"Yes. Necessarily. I need to rule out the possibility that these two events are connected. If Brandon is behind the vandalism, then I'll go one direction. If someone vandalized my showroom because of my connection to the police force, then I'll go another. I can't ignore the situation if my actions impede the investigation."

"What about you? If Tex's investigation impedes your progress in life? Does he get a pass because he's a cop?"

"It's not the same," I said.

"You're right. It's not. But you never struck me as the type who would willfully let her business become a casualty of her partner's job."

Nasty's words stung, mostly because there was a note of truth to them. "You were a cop. Their jobs are bigger than ours." Even as I said it, I felt annoyed at Nasty for pushing me into a corner and mad at Tex for giving her the ammunition to do so.

"Yes, and I left when being a cop stopped being good for me. What I do, running a security business, helps the city of Dallas as much as the cops do, but I do it on my terms. I might not appreciate your wardrobe choices, but I always thought at heart you were a little like me."

There had been too many things in the recent past that were out of my control for Nasty's observations to go unchecked. I didn't know what it was she wanted, and I didn't care. What I needed from her had nothing to do with my lawsuit.

"Tex knows you have a brain and you're not afraid to use it. Does he know you called me for a ride home?"

"No, but that was different. I needed to loop you in."

"Tell yourself whatever story you need to, Madison. I won't judge."

She turned on the radio but almost immediately switched it

off. "Tex can't tell you details about his case. My involvement is different. What do you want to know?"

I studied Nasty's face. Since meeting her, I'd been aware of her confidence and youth. But the pregnancy brought something new. Her confidence was less in-your-face. The impatience that I'd once interpreted as competitive hostility now came across as the direct approach. She was a smart, driven woman living by her own rules in a predominantly male field. She went for what she wanted and didn't complain that opportunities weren't given to her. Here she was, pregnant with the child of a man fifty years her senior, refusing his marriage proposals, and keeping the baby. She had a full staff of trained security techs, but it felt like she was asking me for help.

"I'll take whatever you're willing to share."

"Shira Burr contacted me a month ago. She met me at a party with Gerry, so it was an informal call. She said some confidential information was stolen from her husband's office, and she wanted increased security on the place."

"A man like Winston Burr must already have security measures in place," I said. "I saw his house. He lives behind locked gates a quarter mile back from the road. In a town where houses are built on top of each other, that amount of real estate doesn't come cheap."

"The Burrs have problems, but money isn't one of them. Winston was transparent about his interest in owning the city. He bought property when it suited him, and that doesn't sit well with the city planners who have to deal with him whenever they try to monetize a public property."

"Like White Rock Lake."

"Among others, yes." Nasty slowed to a stop by a red light and uncapped a sleek black S'well canister that sat in the cupholder.

She tipped her head back and drank. The light changed, and she handed the canister to me. I held out my hand for the cap and sealed it back up while she drove.

"I told Shira I'd look into things for her."

"You didn't insist she pay you?"

"Positive word of mouth from the Burrs will get me more than a paycheck tied to a confidentiality agreement. I interviewed her staff even though they'd all been vetted thoroughly by her and felt confident the threats were coming from the outside. I suggested cameras inside the house, but she said no."

"Why was Winston at the lake?"

"The last time Shira saw him, he said he had a meeting. He left shortly after six and never came home. That was a week ago. She showed me his bank statements, and there's been no activity on his credit card for over a week. He didn't show for his meeting, but his assistant said he never called to reschedule."

"What about her?"

"Shira makes running that estate a full-time job. In the past week, she's had two meetings with her charity group on fundraising, appointments with party planners, and trips to check out five potential concert hall rentals. She signed for a Sub-Zero on Tuesday and hosted her book club on Wednesday." Nasty studied me. "Tex knows all of this. I called him about it, and he said Shira gave him full access to both her and Winston's calendars and contacts."

When Tex and I found Winston's body in the trash can, it had been unidentifiable. Time had passed, weather had intervened, and nature had taken its course.

"Who's responsible for emptying the trash by the lake?" I asked suddenly.

Nasty cut her eyes to me and then back to the road. "The city."

"They have a schedule, right? How long had it been since they emptied the trash by the pavilion?"

"Weekly."

"Then those bodies hadn't been there a full week. Can bodies become that unrecognizable in a week?"

"Ask Tex. Depending on the answer, that might be something he'd want to investigate."

I hadn't stopped to think about what resources Nasty had—and didn't have—now that she worked for the private sector. She excelled as a businesswoman, but the badge had given her access to records that were now out of reach.

"You want that life, don't you?" I asked. "Money above all else?"

"Money doesn't make people bad. You know that, right? I'm not bad because I want to live at a certain level, or because I want my child to have unlimited opportunities. I'm not bad because I make decisions in line with my goals to be wealthy."

I couldn't argue with her or tell her she was wrong for wanting more out of life. I'd pinched pennies when Mad for Mod was new, and things got easier after I started booking bigger clients. I hadn't recognized how much I'd been struggling until suddenly, I wasn't.

"You really do have it all," I said.

"I have what I want. It's not the same thing."

"Yes, but you're happy with the life you created. Not a lot of people figure that out."

The conversation lapsed. She turned onto my street and parked alongside the sidewalk by my front door. I never used that door, but I didn't ask Nasty to pull around to the side. I dug out my keys and thanked her for the ride.

"Madison, wait," she said.

I pulled my leg back inside and closed the door. Without the seatbelt, it was easier to face her.

She had her hand on her swollen belly and rubbed in small circles. "I gave you a hard time about living in the past, but the truth is, living in the past is as bad as running from it. The reason I said I'd help you with your business is because I know what it would feel like if someone came after mine. I know you're going to fight for what's yours and not play the victim card. I might not respect the way you dress, but I respect the way you act."

I hadn't expected Nasty to pay me compliments and wasn't sure if compliments were the currency of manipulation. I couldn't discount the feeling that there was something deeper at the core of her motivation this time.

"I can't promise you anything," I said. "But I'll find out what I can."

2 3

I GOT OUT OF THE CAR AND APPROACHED THE BARELY USED entrance. Business cards had been jammed between the door and the frame. They announced reporters who wanted an interview. Brandon had done a number on my reputation, and until the next flavor of the month came around, the media wasn't going to leave me alone. If I opened the door, the cards would fall, indicating I'd been here. I left the door locked and went in through the back door.

AFTER A LONELY NIGHT of sleeping in a quiet, dog-free house, I was thankful when my alarm went off early the next day. A text message had come through overnight: *meet me at the pool*. I pulled on a bathing suit and a coverup, packed a bag, and drove to Crestwood.

Tex and the dogs were waiting for me. Tex in a bathing suit wasn't an unwelcome sight. He kept himself in shape by a combination of activities, though age (and the occasional Lone Star beer) had brought with it a layer of softness over his torso. His arms were thick with muscles that he flexed in the shooting range, and his leg strength came from morning runs on which I'd never join thanks to my thrice-injured knee.

"I didn't expect you to swim today," I said. I pulled my swim cap over my head and tucked my blond hair underneath.

"I'm not here to swim."

I observed his bare chest. "Then you wore the wrong outfit."

He pulled a pair of goggles on over his head and approached the end of the pool. I stood behind him. He turned back to me and lowered his voice. "Do a couple warm-up laps and then take a break."

The thing about morning swims was that, aside from a handful of triathletes and me, the regulars were seniors. I knew some by name. Others had watched me go from broken-hearted to dating Hudson to single again. I'd been approached about set-ups with sons, grandsons, pastors, and even butchers, and always declined. I doubted the seniors were as clueless as Tex wanted to believe, though they remained polite about his occasional presence and never pried about the status of our relationship.

I swam eight laps and glided into the wall. Tex stood in the water by the end of the lane. He looked like he was pausing between sets himself, but his hair was still dry.

"Any reporters see you get home last night?"

"Nope. The bright side of getting home that late is that nobody was awake to notice."

He nodded. "Good. I know you want life to get back to normal. Hang in there, and this'll blow over."

"Thanks," I said. I doubted Tex asked to meet me at the pool so he could check on my mental state, but it was nice that he supported me.

"What are your plans for today?" he asked.

I shrugged. "I was going to help Connie get her record sleeve supplies out of my studio."

"Did she find another home for her workshop?"

"Half of Connie's desire to start a business was to create something like what I had with Mad for Mod. Now that she's seen how quickly it can fall apart, she lost her motivation."

"What about her customers?"

"Someone posted a negative review, and orders have slowed down. I think she's seeing that the reality of being a business owner isn't as glamorous as she originally thought."

"Spending time with Connie sounds like a good idea," he said. "Take your mind off the lawsuit."

"What about you?"

"I'm expecting another full day today, but hopefully I can crash tonight. Come by when your day with Connie ends." He hoisted himself out of the pool, pulled a T-shirt over his wet torso, collected Wojo from the lifeguard station, and left.

No mention of Yasmine Garcia's identity.

No news about the case.

No invitation to the community watch group.

I completed a few additional sets, though my heart wasn't in it. It had been one thing to show up at Tex's investigations by accident, but it was another now that we were dating. If our connection was rooted in chaos, we were doing a fine job of ensuring our relationship's success.

After swimming, I pulled my coverup over my bathing suit, collected Rocky, and drove home to shower and change. Spending the night in my house had felt great, and I was in the mood to tell off a reporter or two if they came knocking on my door.

One of my favorite aspects of buying the estates of newly deceased was learning about the owners. We have a different relationship with the dead when they were strangers to us in life. When you learned about a person not from interactions, but from their possessions, you discovered a porthole to the past. A mean boss, a cheating wife, a lazy coworker all left behind boxes of items that spoke to something unique: their taste.

Among the wardrobe finds in the attic was a dresser packed with pristine Lacoste cardigans from the estate of Craig Marquis. I had an agreement with a local vintage store who bought cartons of men's clothes for a flat fee, and I might have done the same with this except for the delightful shades of Orlon contained within. Craig was a retired lit professor from the University of Texas in Austin in 1964. He favored white turtlenecks, candy-colored cardigans, and plaid trousers all neatly folded in a Broyhill Brasilia high-boy dresser. The top two drawers had been stuffed with dog-eared copies of books by Russian novelists from the mid-nineteenth century. *Crime and Punishment* appeared to have been a favorite.

I pulled on a green V-neck cardigan over a white-and-pink-flowered sleeveless shell and white two-way stretch pants, both of which were closet staples. I laced up green Keds and brewed a fresh pot of coffee in preparation for Connie's arrival.

Half an hour later, Connie parked her aqua Fiat out front. She charged inside my festive yellow kitchen and tossed a stack of catalogs onto the table. "I figured out my future. I'm going to be a florist!" she announced with the same enthusiasm she'd shown with her record sleeve business.

Today Connie was dressed in a shrunken gray T-shirt with an

image of Ziggy Stardust. Cat-eye sunglasses were perched on top of her head. Her blunt cut bob was still wet as if she'd showered recently and let it air dry.

I filled two Eva Zeisel Hallcraft Tri-tone mugs with fresh coffee from my Chemex coffee maker and carried the mugs to the table, then added a small Russel Wright pitcher of milk and a milky yellow WAKU Feuerfest Keramik covered bowl filled with sugar cubes.

"Good morning to you too," I said.

"Sorry. I'm excited." She pulled a white Krispy Kreme box out of her tote bag. "I bought donuts!"

Connie had the same love of mid-century modern objects as I did, and I turned our semi-regular breakfast visits into an excuse to pull out my most loved mismatched pieces. I added two pale-green La Solana plates to the table and extracted a glazed cruller from the donut box. "I thought you were going to be a waitress?"

"I was. That's how this all started. I went back to Mel's Diner to get an application, and I had a piece of peach pie while I was waiting. You know, quality control."

"Sure."

"And I was staring out the window while all these people harassed the waitress, and I thought, 'Connie, you do not want to work at a diner.'"

"It's good you figured that out sooner rather than later," I said.

She finished her donut.

"I suppose it was a hop, skip, and a jump from waitress to florist."

She laughed. "It was more like a jaywalk. I was sitting there with my pie, staring out the window, and it hit me. All those people we saw coming and going from the florist meant one thing."

It certainly meant there would be a lot of DNA confusing Tex's crime scene, though I doubted that was what Connie meant. "What?" I asked.

"Flowers are a recession-proof business. There's demand. Weddings, proms, funerals, restaurants, breakups—"

"Breakups?"

"Sure. I got more flowers after I caught Ned having an affair than I had at our wedding."

"That's charming."

"I know. I was thinking of sending him a big bouquet the day the divorce was final, but I don't know which bloom says, 'screw you.'" She raised her mug and swallowed a few gulps. "Added bonus: if I become a florist, I'll learn the language of flowers. Win-win!"

It was nice to see Connie coming out the other side of the depression she'd entered after learning her hipster husband was having an affair. I was partially responsible for the discovery of the news. Both she and Ned were on my design team, and an unexpected business trip pulled him out of town and left an open position.

The contest rules said that to have a new team member approved, I'd needed proof that we were one man down. Ned's hotel confirmation would have been sufficient, but the charge on the credit card led to the other incriminating facts, the largest two being the absence of a business trip and travel arrangements for his secretary. Connie accused, Ned confirmed, and here we were.

"What will it take to become a florist?" I asked.

"I have no idea." She picked up a second donut and bit into it then brushed crackled crumbs of glaze from the front of her T-shirt. "But it was right there, you know? Like a sign. And it was so easy."

"Did I miss something?"

"Huh?" She looked up at me and set the half-eaten donut down. "Oh, right. I didn't tell you what happened. I dropped my wallet in the parking lot when I left yesterday. At least I thought I did at the time, but it was wedged between the driver's seat and the center console of my car."

I spun my hand in a circle, gesturing for her to get on with the story.

"Right. I thought I dropped my wallet, so I went to the flower shop, and that's when I found out the shop is for sale."

"Akins?" I tried to remember if Arnold had told me they were selling the flower shop, but with everything that had transpired, my conversation with him was a distant memory. "Do you have the money to buy a flower shop?"

"Ned is buying me out of the house, and my lawyer says I'll get a juicy divorce settlement too. I'd like to do something big with the money. Something significant that closes one door and opens another."

Arnold Akins had admitted to me that Winston Burr owned the mortuary and had announced that he was selling to the city, but Arnold hadn't said anything about the flower shop. I doubted the city would have any interest in the property as it was, and lacking the proximity to the public park, there was no value to the location. He'd said that the shop was an add-on business intended to support the mortuary, but without the mortuary, it might not be profitable. Selling now made sense for him. Buying it made sense for Connie.

I watched her press her finger onto the soil of a small African violet I kept on my kitchen ledge. "A flower shop," she said dreamily. "Planting things. Growing things. Having my hands in the dirt all day. Flowers have nothing to do with the music industry, so I won't be reminded of Ned."

Connie tended to be flighty, but I couldn't fault her for indulging in her newfound curiosity. My whole life—business owner, landlord, puppy mother—had come out of a breakup, and the idea to buy an apartment building and then start up Mad for Mod had felt right from the moment it hit me. It was a chapter of my life I hoped never ended. Far be it from me to do anything other than encourage Connie in her pursuit.

Connie tapped the catalogs. "I found four different flower design courses in the area. I have appointments set up with each of them. I don't want to make a rash decision about my future. Want to join me?"

"Sure," I said, happy for the distraction. I flipped through the catalogs. While I'd escorted Tex to the medical examiner to get a positive ID on a body, Connie had been busy. "Does this mean you don't want to get your supplies from my studio today?"

"That's a funny thing. I bought the paper I use to craft record sleeves in bulk, and I thought I was going to have to take a loss on it. Now I can use it to wrap up flower stems. I already have a jump start on what I'll need for my next endeavor. If you don't mind, I'll leave everything there and get it when I'm ready. Hey! I could run my flower shop out of your studio!"

A small part of me wanted to encourage Connie to find her own shop to open, but the less optimistic voice in my head asked why bother? If her circumstances turned out anything like mine, she should minimize her up-front risks so there'd be less to lose when it all fell apart.

OVER THE NEXT TWO HOURS, Connie and I made a tour of flower design schools in the greater Dallas area. The first was run out of a woman's living room, and the second had converted to online lessons. The third was in a sketchy part of town, so we bypassed it in favor of the last one that took place at the Dallas Market Center.

The building, boasting over five million square feet of showroom and rental space, was the home base for various wholesalers predominantly in the fashion, beauty, and decorating businesses. For visitors more interested in history lessons than personal beautification, it was remembered as the destination President Kennedy *didn't* reach thanks to his assassination. These days, I knew it as the home base for Brandon Montgomery Headquarters.

We signed in at security and collected visitor badges then located the flower design school on the directory. I gave Connie a head start and mapped out the location of Montgomery Designs so I could give it a wide berth. Brandon's showroom was on the second floor. I caught up with Connie and confirmed we'd remain on the main level.

Flower Design School, or FDS as the directory called it, was a night course taught in a flower shop called Nate Green Designs. A petite man in a pink shirt with a blue cardigan draped over his shoulders greeted us. "Hello, ladies. Welcome. Fancy a flower?" The man's smile showed off bleached white teeth that contrasted with his George-Hamilton tan. He held a bundle of blooms in one hand and peeled off a stem first for Connie and then for me. She happily took the blossom, but I waved him off.

"What brings you here today? Birthday? Wedding? Dinner party?" the man asked.

"School," Connie said. "I want to learn the art of flower

design." She stepped back and looked up at the sign above the entrance. "Is Nate Green here?"

"I'm Nate!" the man said. His face lit up. "Darlin', you came to the right place. Our next class starts in three weeks, and I have an opening." He set the bundle of flowers on the counter and hurried behind it. He opened a leather-bound planner and ran his finger over the dates until reaching one in the future.

"Three weeks?" she said. Anybody in a thirty-foot radius could hear the dejection in her voice. "I was hoping for something sooner."

"Let me see if we've had any cancelations."

I wandered away while the two of them conducted important flower design school business and scanned the assortment of fresh blooms. A wedding cake table sat in the middle of the room, filled with dark-green tube-shaped vases that held precut stems of daisies, lilies, and other pungent flowers. Fans sat in the corner of the storefront, blowing the scent out into the common area. It was both an advertisement to lure people in and an effective way of keeping the scent from being too cloying in the small space. Even so, I felt the beginning of a headache and moved past the fresh-cut stems to the refrigerated cases of roses.

Inside the walk-in case were roses of every color imaginable. There were the traditional red, yellow, white, and pink in bulk, and peach, light blue, sterling, and green in smaller quantities. Roses in varying levels of color intensity were farther back. I hadn't given much thought to the midnight-blue rose petal that I'd first seen at White Rock Lake, but surrounded with so many color choices, I looked for one like that. Midnight blue was one of the few colors they appeared not to have in stock.

I put my hand on the inside door handle to exit and paused

when I spotted a third person who'd joined Connie and Nate's conversation.

It was Brandon.

I stepped backward, away from the doors, but kept my eyes on him. What had led him down here from his showroom? Had he seen me? This was my second chance encounter with him over two days, and Nasty's words repeated in my mind. He hired a detective to find the dirt under my fingernails, she'd said. Did that mean he was watching my every move?

A second thought occurred to me. Was there more power in going along with his plan to get me? If a detective followed me around for any length of time, he'd soon discover my most incriminating activity was not signaling when I changed lanes.

The cold, damp air inside the refrigerated case had initially felt good but now made my lungs felt wet and heavy. Moisture built up on the interior of the glass, which made observations difficult, but I watched Brandon and Nate talking while Connie moved away. Nate pulled something out of his pocket and handed it to Brandon, who turned and left.

A chill spread over me, turning into uncontrollable shivers. Having gone from the hot, damp weather outside to the chilly refrigerated case inside in a short amount of time left me in need of a decent gulp of dehumidified air. The Orlon cardigan was equivalent to a sweater made from recycled bottles of soda—no help in the warmth department at all. I pushed on the door to exit, but the latch stuck. I jiggled it with decreasing dexterity until it popped loose and the door swung open. I stumbled out and gasped for a deep breath. Connie and Nate turned to me.

"You're not supposed to go in there," Nate said. He pointed to a small sign that said, "Please ask for assistance with roses."

I inhaled and exhaled two more times and then apologized. "I didn't see the sign," I said. "I saw all of the colors and wanted to check if you carried a specific shade."

"We carry every shade you can imagine," Nate said. "What were you looking for. Lavender? Pink and yellow hybrid?"

"Midnight blue," I said. I fumbled in my handbag and pulled out the faded rose petal. "This is a few days old, but it should give you an idea."

Nate's face clouded. "We don't carry midnight-blue roses," he said dismissively.

I stared at the faded rose petal. The intense blue was still visible in the center. For something that had started out so unique and lovely, it was being scorned as if it were too common for consideration. "Is this an exclusive genetic modification offered by another florist?"

"Exclusive? Hardly. Midnight-blue roses don't exist in nature. That was made by dipping a white rose into dark-blue ink. It's a cheap trick used on prom boutonnieres and funeral wreaths."

2 4

NATE CROSSED HIS ARMS. "DID YOU WANT ANYTHING ELSE? MAYBE some carnations with glitter sprayed on them?"

It took everything I had to keep calm. "No, thank you." I gave him my sweetest Doris Day smile. "The roses were for a decorator I know. Brandon Montgomery? He seems like the type to go for something like this." I waved the faded petal between us.

Nate's face reddened. "I know who you are. Get out of my showroom. I don't want your business." He turned to Connie, who was sniffing flowers in a display by the door. "And you. Find another flower institute. This one rejected your application."

"But I haven't applied yet," she said.

"Don't bother."

AFTER BEING evicted from the flower shop, Connie and I grabbed a healthy lunch at Flower Child, an organic restaurant that promised food enlightenment. Connie ordered the Glow Bowl, and I had the Forbidden Rice. I can't say I felt more enlightened when we finished, but I did feel full.

I drove Connie back to my place. An unusual number of cars were in the neighborhood, and until I approached my house and saw a crew of reporters camping out on my front yard, I didn't realize the traffic congestion was because of me. I dropped Connie off and remained in the car until she drove away, then followed her to the stop sign. She turned left, and I turned right. My Alfa Romeo had most likely been spotted, but if I didn't stop, the reporters couldn't harass me.

My phone rang with an unfamiliar number that I screened. After a voicemail alert, I discovered a message from Arnold Akins to call him at my earliest convenience. It was as convenient a time as any, so I did.

"Akins Funeral and Mortuary," he answered.

"Arnold, this is Madison Night. You left me a message?"

"Yes. Madison, hi. I, well, listen. I'll cut to the chase. Remember when you offered to help us out for a few days? Dad's been making a real mess of things around here. It's like he wants to sabotage what's left of the business. I can't keep him in line and do everything else I need to do by myself. Does your offer still stand?"

"What do you have in mind?" I asked.

"We have a funeral service this Saturday, and between the phones, the room set-up, and the flower order, I can't tell which end is up. He managed to break both the incinerator and the refrigeration coil in the flower closet, and it sure would help if you could manage the front for a few hours so I could get some work done. Am I asking too much?"

"I'd welcome the distraction."

"Great! Great. Come by whenever you can. The door is open."

It was a ten-minute drive to the funeral home. The parking lot was empty. I found Arnold in the hallway surrounded by flower arrangements.

"Madison," he said. Sweat dampened his forehead, and he used the back of his shirt sleeve to blot it. "You're a lifesaver."

"And you're . . . what are you doing with all those flowers?"

"These are to get us through the weekend services. We bring them onsite a day early to make it easier to set the room, but the flowers need to be in a temperature-controlled, humid environment."

"If that closet was temperature controlled, you wouldn't be sweating," I observed.

"The A/C coil broke. I'm going to have to take the flowers home and refrigerate them overnight."

I couldn't help noticing the clammy temperature inside the building. Small oscillating fans had been placed in the corners, but they merely pushed uncomfortably humid air back and forth. I picked up a brochure and fanned myself. "I can't tell if I'm having a hot flash or if it's warm in here," I said.

"As if the closet wasn't enough, Acie's on the fritz again, and Quinn's not answering his phone."

"Quinn?"

"The A/C repairman. You met him the other day. It's like he knows if I'm desperate, I'll pay extra." Arnold's plaid shirt was unbuttoned at the neck, revealing a white cotton undershirt. I doubted the layered effect helped him manage the humidity, but also recognized his need to look professional for prospective clients.

"Is his number out front?"

"His contact info is on the computer in a file called 'Address Book.' Probably in the list of recently opened files. If you can't reach him, you might need to find someone else who can get here today. You wouldn't happen to know a handyman, would you?"

"As a matter of fact, I know several," I said.

I went to the front desk and called Quinn. As suspected, the call went to voicemail. I identified myself and left a callback number, and then called Hudson's cell.

"Hey, lady," he answered.

"Hey." We exchanged pleasantries, and then I got down to business. "I'm helping out at Akins Funeral and Mortuary, and their A/C is on the fritz. You wouldn't want to pick up some easy money while you're in town, would you?"

"Air conditioning repair isn't exactly easy," he said with a chuckle, "but I admire your salesmanship. I'll swing by this afternoon."

I gave him the details and hung up. In one sense, calling Hudson to schedule a job felt familiar. Like the old days, when I was a decorator, he was my handyman, and murder was the plot of the book on my nightstand. So much had changed since then that the feeling of familiarity quickly dissipated, replaced by anxiety that the house of cards in which I was trying to live was about to be blown over by a strong gust of air.

I kept myself busy with admin tasks: typing up client files, sending notices for more past-due invoices, and stopping payment on Quinn's check. When five o'clock rolled around, I left the desk and checked in with Arnold.

"How's it going?" I asked.

"Would be a lot better if the air conditioning were working. Are you sure your guy is coming?"

"He's reliable. I sprang this on him, so I don't know what his schedule looked like, but he won't let you down."

"Okay. Call me when he gets here, and I'll show him where the unit is."

I scanned the room. The chairs were lined up neatly, six rows of seven, all facing the front of the room, where two easels sat. One held an enlarged yearbook photo of a young, pretty Mexican woman. The other was empty.

"Is that Yasmine Garcia?" I asked. "I recognize the photo from the newspaper."

"Yes," he said. "Shame what happened to her. We barely had a chance to know her."

My brows pulled together as I tried to parse his words. "She was young," I said. "It's always sad when someone dies before their lives get started."

"Yasmine was married and had two kids. She was well on her way to having a nice life. I meant the flower shop. She started working for us last month."

I felt that familiar burst of adrenaline. There was a reason for her to be at Akins Flowers: her job. Thanks to the loan, Winston Burr was the new owner of all the Akins's properties. Was this it? The connection between two victims? Did Tex know about this?

While my mind was racing off in another direction, Arnold kept talking. I tuned back in to the conversation mid-sentence. "...less than a month ago. Taking orders, making local deliveries, that sort of thing. I told Dad we should bring her on here to help with the place, but he didn't like the idea. Said he didn't want another person nosing around the joint and to leave her with the flowers."

"Did your dad dislike her?"

"I don't think it had anything to do with Yasmine. The last time there was a woman here, it was my mom. Dad doesn't want anybody to try to fill her shoes."

"Where's your dad now?"

"Outside mowing the lawn. It's the reality of owning a mortuary. This rain makes things difficult, but we get complaints when the grounds are let go. Dad's got a riding mower, but it's still going to take twice as long as usual."

We stared at the picture of Yasmine, and our conversation lapsed into silence. This was the same photo I'd seen in the paper. Like all yearbook photos, this one lacked warmth and personality. Surely Officer Garcia could have come up with something better than this?

I pointed to the other easel. "Are you expecting another photo?"

"No, that's for the funeral wreath." As soon as the words were out of Arnold's mouth, his face went red. "The funeral wreath. We don't have a funeral wreath!"

"Tell me where it is, and I'll get it."

"That's just it. We make them up at the flower shop, but the flower shop's been closed by the police. I forgot all about it."

"I think I can help you out with this one too," I said.

An hour later, I parked in the lot outside By George. Placing a last-minute order for a funeral wreath could have been handled over the phone, but this gave me the perfect excuse to check in with George to see how her deposition had gone. I entered the building and was greeted by one of her assistants. George sat at a small round table with a prospective client and a woman I guessed to be the client's mother. They had matching gold charm bracelets and blond hair.

George looked up and smiled but continued with her consultation. I popped next door to a Oaxacan restaurant and placed a takeout order for dinner. By the time I returned to the wedding planning showroom, the clients were saying goodbye. I milled around while they finished up. George joined me next to a display of purple silk hydrangeas.

"Madison," George said. "I see you as much now as I did when you worked here."

"And this time I have a job for you." I told her about my need for the wreath and explained the reason for the last-minute request.

"For anybody else, I'd say no," she said. "But I feel a little guilty about what happened, so I'll whip something up."

"Don't," I said immediately.

"I thought you needed it?"

"I mean don't feel guilty," I said. "You did what you did for your business. You're not at fault."

George exhaled noticeably. "I sure am glad to hear you say that. Honestly, I feel like my business got caught in the crosshairs of Mad for Mod vs. Montgomery Designs, and I just want it all to be over."

I felt a nauseous feeling in my stomach as if I'd eaten a burrito with bad meat. "Is that what you said at your deposition?"

"Yes," she said reluctantly. She put her hand on my arm. "But I told them you did what I asked. I said you executed Brandon's design to the letter. I told them I'd be happy to recommend Mad for Mod to anybody considering a renovation."

The more George talked, the worse I felt. I thanked George for squeezing in the order and arranged to pick it up the next morning. I picked up the takeout order and returned to Akins Funeral and Mortuary. The temperature inside the building was refreshing and dry, which told me I'd missed Hudson's trip to get the A/C unit in working order.

Edward Akins was inside the office, relaxing behind the desk. "Nice fella, that Hudson," he said. "Did the job and fixed the incinerator too. Left us a list of contacts for the next time we need some work done. Speaks highly of you. I offered to make him our regular guy, but he said he doesn't live around here anymore."

"He's back in town for a short while," I said. The truth was, I didn't know how long Hudson would be in Dallas or whether I'd see him again. It felt like I was forcing a friendship where one had once been, and again I felt the ground shifting underneath me like tectonic plates. I pulled a foil-wrapped order of tamales and containers of salsa, guajillo rice, refried beans, and queso out of the delivery bag and set it on the desk. "Arnold hasn't eaten all day, and I don't know if you have either. There was a Oaxacan restaurant next to the florist where I ordered the wreath, so I picked up food in case."

Edward peeked inside and groaned. "More of that snooty downtown food," he said derisively. He looked up at me. "I told my son I wanted a pizza."

2 5

BETWEEN TRAIPSING AROUND DALLAS WITH CONNIE, WORKING WITH Arnold, and spending time with George, it had been another long day. The last time Tex and I spoke, he was with the medical examiner. I knew better than to bother him with a just-checking-in phone call while he was on a case, but he had invited me to come over.

I drove to his townhouse. I'd missed Rocky's company last night, and while Tex's townhouse was a playground for the dogs, tonight I wanted Rocky with me.

The Jeep was in the garage. I parked in Tex's driveway and walked around to the front, ringing the bell to announce my presence. Two different barks comingled on the other side of the door. I listened for Tex's footsteps to descend the stairs, but other than happy yipping, I heard nothing.

I pulled out my phone and called Tex. His distinctive ringtone sounded from inside. The call went to voice mail. I tried again twice with no answer.

Seven months ago, I'd decorated Tex's spare bedroom, and I'd yet to give back his key. I flipped through my keychain to his and let myself in.

"Tex? It's me," I announced. I bent down to ruffle the fur on each of the dogs' heads and climbed up the stairs. "Where are you?"

Tex lived in a three-story townhouse. The bottom floor had guest quarters. Up the stairs lay the kitchen, dining, and spare bedrooms, and above that were the master bedroom, bathroom, and a small office. Above that, not part of the square footage, was the rooftop deck. Dallas temperatures being what they were, the deck sounded better in concept than it felt in humidity, but every once in a while, the stars aligned and a night spent lounging on the rooftop was a luxury unparalleled.

After I climbed the stairs, I saw evidence of Tex's presence in the kitchen. A cap from a Lone Star beer sat next to an old laptop and a case file. His phone rested not far from the computer, still glowing with the announcement of my missed call.

"Tex?" I called again.

I heard a toilet flush above me, and then footsteps. Having a case while being ill couldn't be fun, but the demands of an investigation didn't go on pause because of a sore throat or allergies. Tex was burning the candle at both ends, and he must be exhausted. He didn't need to make time for me.

I removed my cardigan and draped it over a barstool. I set the evidence bags on the counter, tossed Tex's beer cap into his recycling bin, and walked to the base of the stairs. "Hey," I called up. "I'm here to get Rocky."

There was no answer.

I clipped Rocky's leash on and went back to the kitchen. A quick scan of Tex's cabinets and cupboard indicated he wasn't at all prepared to feed his fever, or allergies, or anything else that didn't require dry grains or prepackaged beans. Tex ate out a lot, mostly because the job required him to fit meals between investigative and office work. The dining community was generous to the police, but I wondered what he subsided on when left alone. Navy beans and orzo?

Snooping in Tex's food storage was a distraction from the file on the counter. After having announced my presence, I expected Tex to drag himself downstairs in whatever state he was in simply to keep me from nosing around. But the more time that passed, the more I heard Nasty's voice in my ear. Asking for a favor.

I would have liked to banish that thought with the knowledge that I owed her nothing, but the truth was, I owed her a lot. Not for the help with the lawsuit, but with a recent situation where my life was in danger. And for investing in a project of mine when I needed capital. And for recognizing when Tex was in trouble that holding a grudge over a breakup was the last thing required.

He left it sitting out. He invited me over. He knew I'd get Rocky. He heard me come in. He's not stopping me.

By the time I looked at the pages, I'd convinced myself Tex left the file open because he wanted my opinion.

I flipped past the police report—information I probably already knew—and arrived at Lloyd's contribution to the file. It was a generic form with a drawing of a naked man facing forward and backward. Lloyd had made notes by the neck and torso indicating scratches. Another notation was made by the top side of the head. By "Cause of Death" he'd written, "trauma to the skull."

If trauma to the skull had led to death, then what was with the scratches?

I was so lost in the file that I almost missed the sound of the key turning in the lock downstairs. The dogs barked, first Wojo and then Rocky. Wojo ran down the staircase, and Rocky strained against the leash that was looped around my wrist.

"Hey there, little buddy," Tex said. "Yo, Night, you here?"

If Tex had been out, then who was upstairs?

I flipped the folder closed and moved silently to the top of the stairs. Tex ascended, cradling Wojo and rubbing the fur on the puppy's head. I held my finger up to my mouth and then pointed up. "We're not alone," I whispered. "There's someone upstairs."

Tex thrust Wojo at me and went through the living room and up the second flight of stairs that led to his bedroom. I stayed with the dogs with one hand on the phone. Tex's feet carried him up again, to the rooftop. About a minute later, he came back down.

"Was that a joke?" He sneezed and then glanced at the kitchen counter behind me. "If you were trying to cover your tracks, you did a lousy job."

I looked at the open file folder and then back at Tex. "I did not imagine this," I said. I set Wojo down, looped Rocky's leash around the kitchen faucet, and passed Tex. "There were footsteps. And a toilet flush."

This time I led the way upstairs. I arrived in Tex's bedroom with him on my heels. The bed was made, and the room appeared exactly as Tex usually left it. There was nothing to indicate I was telling the truth.

"Night, if this was an excuse to get me into the bedroom, you could have asked."

I ignored Tex's somewhat expected comment and climbed the stairs to the rooftop deck. The door opened onto a dusky sky and a wave of humidity.

"Where can you go from here?"

"Back inside."

"No," I said. "Whoever I heard in your bedroom had to come

up here when they heard me come in. Where could they go?" I looked at the adjoining rooftop deck. "How hard is it to climb to your neighbor's deck?"

"You're certain you heard someone?"

"I'm certain I heard someone."

Tex went to the ledge and scanned the surrounding alleys. He moved to the other side and did the same before turning back to me.

"Unless the perp was one of my neighbors, he'd have to break into one of the townhouses and exit through the front or back door. It's late, and it's still close to a hundred degrees. Nobody's hanging out on their rooftops tonight."

I wiped a tendril of sweat away from my hairline. Tex was right. After five minutes, I was ready to go inside and take an ice bath.

Tex opened the door and stood back to let me go first, and that was when I heard the front door shut.

Wojo, who'd followed us upstairs, barked twice and took off down the staircase. Tex's ladies-first gesture was forgotten as he charged down behind the puppy. I moved slower—down was harder than up—and stopped when I reached the kitchen. Whether or not Tex caught the intruder was one thing, but the absence of the case file I'd left on the counter was another thing altogether.

I'D WANTED TO BE WRONG, BUT THE MISSING FILE SPOKE VOLUMES. This wasn't a random break-in. Whoever the intruder was, he or she was connected to the homicide investigation.

I sat on the sofa with Rocky and Wojo and waited for Tex to return. It didn't take long. The front door shut, and his footsteps sounded on the carpeted stairs. When he appeared on the landing, he was empty handed.

He went to his refrigerator and pulled out two bottles of beer. He uncapped both and joined me in the living room, handing me one. The amber liquid was cool and refreshing after experiencing the heatwave on the roof, but it would take more than a cold beer to remove the tension.

"Did you see anybody?" I asked.

Tex shook his head. "It's getting dark out there. Somebody could have jumped into a parked car and either taken off or stayed put and hid in plain sight."

"Did you look inside the parked cars?"

"In the first five I saw, yes. But the West End Shopping Center is two blocks away, and this time of night the lot's full. Bars and restaurants valet for their patrons. Ride share drivers and taxis hang around the area and make it easy for people who drink too much to get a ride home."

"Which means the cars in the lot could have been there for longer than tonight," I said.

"Right."

"And whoever was inside your house could have easily caught a ride share to get out of here in a hurry."

"Right again."

Tex sank onto the sofa beside me and ruffled Rocky's fur. I'd left his leash attached to his collar, but now I unclipped it and let him jump down. He joined Wojo, and the two of them flopped onto a shearling dog bed that Tex had set up in the corner.

"How are you feeling?" I asked.

"Not good. I'd kill for an effective decongestant, but I can't afford to be knocked out." He pulled a wad of tissues from the box on his coffee table and blew his nose then discarded them in an overflowing wastebasket.

"Where were you?" I asked.

He looked confused.

"When I got here. Your Jeep is in your garage, and your phone was on the counter. When I heard the footsteps and the flush I assumed it was you."

"I went to the cemetery," he said. "I needed time to think."

The entrance to Greenwood Cemetery was about fifty yards from Tex's front door. It was home to some of Dallas's oldest family members, along with soldiers from both union and confederate sides. The first time I went to the cemetery, it was with Tex. He showed me the grave of his grandfather and relayed the troubled history within his family.

Since then, when I spent the night at Tex's, I sometimes got up early and went for a walk there myself, pausing to read the gravestones, muse about the families who were interred, and find peace within my sometimes crowded mind. I wasn't surprised to learn that Tex had done the same thing. If peace couldn't be obtained via Nyquil, then he'd take other measures.

He leaned forward and put his head in his hands. "Did you read the file?"

We'd been through versions of this conversation enough times to know how it would end. I saved us some time. "Yes. Not the whole thing, but I saw the medical examiner's report."

I felt the wall of cop energy build up inside him. "Night—"

I put my hand on his arm. "Don't do this, Tex."

He glared at me.

"If we want to have a relationship, then we're going to have to figure out how to handle things like this. You telling me not to get involved doesn't work. Not when I found one of the bodies. Not when I find intruders in your apartment. Not when evidence from your crime scene gets stuck on the bottom of my shoe. Our worlds are too small. They're going to keep getting mixed up. We're like peanut butter and chocolate." I smiled.

"I want you to be safe."

"You can't lock me up in the attic."

"That's not what I want, and you know it."

"My role in life is not to be your foil. I happen to be in a unique situation where I can't do my job."

"How much effort have you put into my investigation so far?"

"Not nearly as much as you think."

Tex called the police department, and about fifteen minutes later, two patrol officers arrived. I brewed a pot of coffee while Tex walked them through his townhouse and told them what he suspected. When the coffee was done, I defrosted a package of chicken breasts and added them to a large pot of water with salt and pepper. Hot chicken soup and coffee were the last things I craved on a hundred-degree night in Dallas, but neither was for me.

While I brought the water to a boil, Tex and the officers returned to the living room. They didn't try to hide their conversation, but they didn't broadcast information either. I pulled three mugs from the cabinet and filled them, then put them on a tray and carried them to the men.

"Sanders, Goosehaven, this is Madison Night. She was the one who first heard the intruder."

I nodded at the officers. "Fresh coffee?" I asked.

They each took a mug.

Goosehaven, the leaner of the two men, raised his mug. "Thank you, ma'am." He held the mug to his head and inhaled but didn't drink. He lowered the mug and asked, "Can you walk us through what happened here tonight?"

"Sure," I said. "I came to pick up my dog. When Captain Allen didn't answer the door or his phone, I let myself in." I turned to Tex and he nodded. "I have a key from a decorating job I did here several months ago." Goosehaven nodded as if no further explanation about my entry was required. "I called out to Tex to let him know it was me."

"Any reason you didn't take your dog and leave?" Sanders asked. With each word he spoke, the scent of coffee on his breath hit me in short, acidic punches.

"It didn't seem right to let myself in and not check on the captain. I knew he wasn't feeling well and thought I'd see if there was anything I could get for him."

Sanders nodded as if my explanation was acceptable. I didn't know either of these cops, and I didn't know how much Tex had told them about our relationship. So far, my impression had been that he preferred not to answer questions about us at all, keeping our lives separate from his job, but I was getting a distinctly different sense now.

Goosehaven raised his mug to his face again. This time he closed his eyes and inhaled. I watched the rise of his chest and then the fall as he exhaled. He lowered the mug. "Ms. Night, how did you discover Captain Allen wasn't here?"

"He came home," I said. "I heard a toilet flush over my head and I heard footsteps. I assumed he'd been in bed resting, or that he'd be down in a moment. I called up to him to let him know I was here. His phone was on the counter, as was evidence that he'd been enjoying a beer. I had no reason to believe he'd left the dogs alone."

Goosehaven raised the mug and smelled it again.

"Is there something wrong with the coffee?" I asked.

"I'm off caffeine," he said. "Had a couple tachycardia episodes in the past month, and my follow-up physical is scheduled for this week. I'm not taking any chances."

I took the mug from his hand and carried it to the kitchen, where I dumped the contents in the sink. I pulled a clean glass from the cabinet and filled it with decaf iced tea from the refrigerator, then carried the glass back to the group and handed it to him. "This may not wake you up, but it'll eliminate temptation."

"Thank you." Goosehaven emptied the glass in four gulps and set it on the counter. "Ms. Night, Captain Allen tells us you're embroiled in a lawsuit that may have led to vandalism of your business earlier today. Any chance this was all about you?"

I GLARED AT TEX. HE SHRUGGED AND DRANK HIS COFFEE. STEAM rose from the stock pot behind him, and I left the group and stirred the boiling soup and added a pinch of salt before answering.

"I can't see how it could be about me. No one knew I was coming. The intruder was here when I arrived, and the one thing missing is the case file that was sitting on the counter."

The men exchanged glances. "How do we know you didn't take the case file?" Sanders asked.

"For what reason would I do that?"

"To help someone who shouldn't see that information."

"Like who?"

Tex answered. "Like Nasty."

This, I hadn't expected. Donna had asked me to retrieve information for her. I discounted the possibility that she'd been the one in Tex's townhouse, though I knew she'd once been welcome and didn't know if she, too, had a key. Later, I'd strongly suggest that Tex change his locks.

"I didn't take the case file. Not for me, not for Donna Nast."

"Did you read the contents of the file?"

"Yes."

"Why?"

"I'm a curious person."

"You seem like a smart woman, Ms. Night. I'm going to assume you knew what that file was. Why did you read it?"

"I wanted to see the medical examiner's report."

Sanders and Goosehaven exchanged glances. "And?" Sanders prompted.

"And then Captain Allen came in. I told him there was someone else in the house. We both went upstairs to investigate, and by the time we returned to the kitchen, the intruder and the file were missing."

I could see how it looked. If they believed I was working with Nasty, then they could make the argument that I lied about an intruder to get Tex upstairs so Nasty could come in and steal the file. If I hadn't heard the sounds from within the townhouse myself, I might have seen things as suspiciously as they did.

The question about Nasty's interest remained, but I kept it to myself.

"Officers, I know little more than I knew when I entered Captain Allen's townhouse earlier tonight. Specifically, I learned that the cause of death of both victims was blunt force trauma to the head. I was reading the notes Lloyd left in the margins of his report when the captain returned, and at that point my attention shifted to the intruder."

They all stared at me.

"I'd be happy to answer any additional questions you have, but I've told you all I know."

Tex was the first to speak. "Thanks for coming over," he said to the men. "Let me know if you find out anything."

"Sure will," Sanders said. He bent down and hung his hand in front of Wojo, who'd been sniffing at his feet. "Cute dog. What is he? Part chihuahua?"

"Chihuahua-Shi Tzu mix," I said.

"Never heard of that combination before." He straightened up and set his mug on the counter. "Thanks, Captain. We'll be in touch if we find anything." The officers left.

Something about the interaction with the two cops had bothered me from the moment they came in, and I still couldn't shake the sense that this was no routine follow-up. I knew many of the officers in Tex's precinct, and both Sanders and Goosehaven were unfamiliar.

As Wojo hopped around their feet, they had ignored him. Wojo was short for Wojciehowicz, one of the cops on Barney Miller. When Wojo's mother had her litter of puppies, sired by Rocky, the police force had adopted them. Yet Sanders and Goosehaven appeared to have no familiarity with the puppy.

"Which precinct were they from?" I asked Tex.

He turned his back on me and carried the empty coffee mugs to the sink.

"I'm fairly certain they don't work for the Lakewood PD with you, and I'm sure you have your reasons for turning to a different police department for assistance. I understand there's no real reason for you to tell me why, but a simple internet search would surely turn up an answer. I don't think you're at risk of giving away confidential information."

Tex sighed. He opened the lid of the stockpot and inhaled the scent of soup, which wafted across the room and met me in the living room. I hadn't eaten much today, and despite the unseasonableness of it, the soup smelled good.

"Leave it," I said. "It won't be ready for another thirty minutes at best."

Tex replaced the lid and crossed his arms. "Sanders and Goosehaven work for the Dallas Police Department."

"Why was the DPD here? You live in Lakewood. This is your precinct."

"That's right. But my team is taxed with the homicide and vandalism on Greenville. This break-in needs to be treated delicately considering the case file was taken. I don't want anybody to say I was negligent, and the best way to be transparent about what happened was to contact a different police force to investigate."

"You think someone will say that?"

"Sit down, Night."

I filled a mug of fresh coffee for myself and topped off Tex's as well. We sat on the sofa, and I waited for him to talk.

"This is a high-profile case. Whoever murdered Winston Burr knew this was going to be all over the news."

"What about Yasmine Garcia? How does she fit in?"

He didn't seem surprised that I knew. "You found out about her from the file," he guessed incorrectly.

"No, I found out about her from Nasty."

He raised his eyebrows. "You do manage to ferret out information, don't you?"

"What can I say? People tell me things. They think I'm harmless."

He leaned back and extended his arms over the back of the sofa. "Tomorrow morning I'm going to hold a press conference to release

Yasmine Garcia's identity. It wasn't how I'd planned to release the information, but without knowing who took that file, I don't have another choice. I can't afford a leak that makes us look inept."

"What will you say?"

"I'll tell the public that Yasmine Garcia was a twenty-seven-year-old mother of two who recently started work at a local flower shop. I'll say she was an active member of her community and church and that we were investigating her death in conjunction with the murder of Winston Burr. I'll tell them that we have no leads to connect the two, but we're not ruling anything out. And everything I say will be true."

"But?"

"But Yasmine Garcia walked out on her husband two weeks ago. Since then she ran up twenty-four thousand dollars in debt and filed for a permit to carry a concealed weapon."

"Yasmine Garcia had a gun?"

Tex shook his head. "She applied for a permit, but it's still in processing. Seems whatever threat Yasmine wanted to protect against got to her first."

"Yasmine was scared of something," I said. "She had two young boys, and she wanted to protect them."

Tex shook his head. "She left the boys with Garcia when she left. He's been covering for her. Says he left messages with every person he could think of to ask her to come home."

"Where's Garcia now? You hired Imogene to cover the front desk. That indicates you don't expect him back anytime soon."

"Officer Garcia is at something of a crossroads. I told him to take some time off."

"Paid?"

"Not this time."

I shuddered at the images that I'd seen in the police file. My heart swelled for the two young boys who'd lost their mother. They were victims too. Garcia had been nothing but nice to me and Rocky. I had a hard time picturing him driving his wife away, but I wasn't naïve enough to discount a dark side because he kept puppy treats in his desk.

"How'd he take it?"

"As well as can be expected. No matter what Garcia is feeling, he has to take care of the boys. Child protection services are investigating him."

"What does your gut say?"

"Garcia's not our guy."

Tex lapsed into silence. I went to the kitchen to stir the soup. I enhanced the chicken stock with a sprig of thyme, salt, and pepper. I stirred the stock and put the lid back in place.

Tex was a tough but fair boss. He understood the needs of his police officers because he'd been one himself, but he also knew the city needed a kinder, gentler police force to protect them. His job had become a tightrope act, maintaining authority and enforcing the law while getting people to trust them.

When fundraising became a necessary (and regular) aspect of his job, he'd had to relinquish control of his officers' actions. Training and trust were the bedrock, and swift responses to anyone stepping out of line were the pillars of his team. He was short on men and hadn't wanted to suspend Garcia, but inaction and a public outcry of criticism would have been worse. He acted decisively, and Garcia had understood.

"What other leads do you have?"

"We haven't found the clothes or shoes from the victims. Most likely, the killer stripped them at the flower shop and took everything from the scene. Best case scenario, we'll find the garments in the house of a suspect, and that'll seal the case. Worst case, the clothes were incinerated."

"The mortuary has an incinerator for cremations," I said. "You probably know that."

"And half of the residents around White Rock Lake have an outdoor grill. That's a hard avenue to explore."

"What about the rest of the trash in the bin? Underneath the bodies?"

"Mulch. Aside from the flower petal and ribbon, this was the cleanest crime I've seen." He tipped his head back and stared at the ceiling.

"Why two victims?" I asked. "If this was about Yasmine, then why was Winston killed? And if it was about Winston, then why kill Yasmine? They don't seem to have a lot in common."

Tex didn't look at me. I was used to his cop face, the one that showed no emotion. I was familiar with the expression that said, "stay out of this," the one that said, "that's a silly outfit," and the one that said, "do you want to go to the bedroom?" but avoiding eye contact was new. Tex didn't shy away from confrontation. Whatever it was he didn't want to tell me, he was wrestling with something inside him to determine what to do.

"Remember that used condom we found?" he asked.

"Yes. Have you been holding out on me?"

He smiled. "Lloyd swabbed it and got a DNA match to an ex-con out on parole."

I sat forward. "That's good news, right?"

"His parole officer says he cleaned up his act after his last violation. He went to trade school and took a job at—" Tex leaned forward and picked up his beer bottle. He held it by the neck and stared into the opening. He set the bottle back down and shook his head. "He took a job working for a local air conditioning repair company. It was over a hundred before the rain hit, and even with that, it's still in the nineties. This is A/C repair's busy season. Might be coincidence."

Tex didn't believe in coincidence. He told me once that no cops did. It was a construct of people who were too lazy to work for answers to life's mysteries, and in the cops' line of work, a life mystery often meant discovering how someone had died.

"It's Quinn, isn't it?" I asked.

Tex glared at me.

"What? I told you there was an air conditioning repair man out by the mortuary. And the hikers who found Yasmine Garcia reported seeing that van the day they found the body. And you don't believe in coincidence."

"It's Quinn. We delivered the search warrant earlier today. The evidence team is combing over his van as we speak."

Now I knew why he hadn't returned Arnold Akins's calls. "Did he give you a hard time?"

"No, he cooperated. Admitted to being out at the park with his girlfriend last week. Said they got a little frisky in the van after looking at back issues of *Playboy*. Everything matches up with the evidence. Guy like that likes the taste of freedom. Sounded more like bragging than lying."

I sat back and pondered what this meant. It would probably be hard to hide evidence from the van even if it had been professionally cleaned. I said as much to Tex.

"There's a possibility Quinn could have had the van detailed, but this type of crime creates evidence at every turn. DNA, skin flakes, sweat, dirt, flower petals, the list goes on. Whoever killed Ms. Garcia and Mr. Burr did us a favor by moving the bodies." He sneezed.

"Those allergies are killing you," I said.

"I'll survive."

"Your eyes were red earlier today. And last night you had a headache. And now you're sneezing."

"What's your point?"

I held the palm of my hand against Tex's forehead and, after confirming his uncharacteristically hot temperature, put distance between us. "You don't have allergies," I said. "You're sick."

"I'm not sick. I don't get sick." Tex sat back and stretched his arms out on either side of the back of the sofa. I was far enough away from him to know it had more to do with the muscles in his shoulders and neck than any attempts to initiate something physical. (Tex shifted gears in that category way faster than I did, but I'd learned to read the signs.)

"You have two victims. The evidence, which is slim, indicates the murder took place at the flower shop. The bodies were cleaned and moved to the park where they were left for an undetermined amount of time before being discovered."

"In the rain," Tex added. Until he spoke, I wasn't sure if he was paying attention to my recap or if he'd fallen asleep.

"Right. In the rain."

"As if everything else hadn't made this case nearly impossible, the rain was the topper. I'd like to bring Mother Nature up on accessory charges." Tex stood and carried the beer bottles to the kitchen. "How long until that soup is done?"

I followed him. "I'll handle the soup. You should relax."

"I can't relax."

"You're going to get worse if you keep burning the candle at both ends." I lifted the lid of the stockpot and stirred the bubbling broth. "Go take a power nap. I'll toss in some vegetables and call you in about half an hour." I put my hands on his shoulders and turned him around and then tapped the seat of his jeans to send him on his way.

"Careful, Night. I'm too tired to perform." He flashed me a delirious grin, and I rolled my eyes.

I'd expected him to go upstairs and lie down in his bed, but he stretched out on the sofa. It didn't take long to hear steady breathing.

There was something freeing about the task of making chicken soup. It was a recipe I'd watched my mom make before she died, and I found it in an old cookbook when I liquidated their estate. As a single woman, I'd gotten used to shopping for what I needed to minimize post-expiration date food waste, and I often bought lunch from one of the many restaurants on Greenville and lived off the leftovers for dinner the same night. When pressed for time, Lean Cuisine came to my rescue.

But tonight, it felt good to work in the kitchen. Making soup from scratch had nothing to do with my recent troubles. The answers wouldn't be found at the bottom of a stockpot, but a different peace of mind might. I sampled the soup directly from the ladle, added a few extra twists of fresh cracked pepper, and turned it to simmer while I boiled water for egg noodles.

Tex stirred. He rolled onto his back and rubbed his eyes and then sat up and stared at me. "I didn't know you did this," he said.

"Did what?"

"Domesticity."

"I'm not without some talent."

He came into the kitchen and stirred the pot of broth. "If the smell is any indication, I'd say you're being modest."

I pulled two bowls out of the cabinet and set them on the counter next to the stockpot then added a wedge of noodles into each. "It's another use for math."

"Math? I expected you to say it was creativity."

"Sure, there's some creativity involved, but mostly arithmetic. Ratio of water to chicken, addition of salt and pepper. Dividing the noodles into the bowls."

"Subtraction of bones."

"Right." I handed him a bowl. "The perfect dinner multiplied by two."

"You never stop surprising me."

We stood on opposite sides of the counter and ate. It was later than I'd usually have dinner, but I was starved. Tex appeared to be too. Not for the first time, I wondered what his life was like when I wasn't around: prioritizing his investigation over his health, bumping things like food and sleep for the search for information.

"I can help you, you know," I said quietly. I stared into my soup, afraid to see the expression on his face.

He looked up, and a shock of hair fell onto his forehead. "I need you to act like you don't know anything. I need you to go about business as usual."

We finished eating in silence. I rinsed the bowls out and placed them in the dishwasher then dried my hands on a towel.

"There is no business as usual for me, and you know that. My life is about mid-century modern design. I drive around Dallas looking for curbside treasures. I go to the studio and either meet with clients, rearrange the inventory, or catch up on eBay auctions, blogs, and *Atomic Ranch*. Before you came along I swam in the morning, spent my days at the studio, went home for dinner, and was in bed by nine."

"You've been involved in five of my cases," he said. "Five times you dropped everything to nose around where you shouldn't have been."

"Whoa," I said, holding up both hands. "Every one of those times, I had legitimate business that led me to quote-unquote nose around, and you know that. And more than once I called you the moment I knew I'd stepped into something that was your territory."

"Point taken." He sat back and stared at his coffee table. It was glass and chrome, standard issue for a bachelor who traded up from two paint cans and a slab of wood. Tex's whole townhouse was a reminder of his single days. The leather sofa, the modular entertainment center, and the stereo that cost more than everything else combined. His living quarters were as much him as mine were me, and we both silently accepted that.

"You need your rest. I'll finish cleaning up down here. We can figure something out in the morning."

"You're trying to get me into bed," he said. His voice was groggy, and the need for sleep was visible in his face. I'd seen Tex become obsessive when it came to solving a case, going so far as to conduct overnight surveillance while on voluntary hiatus. He took the safety of Lakewood seriously and pushed himself too hard to get answers.

"I *am* trying to get you into bed. Alone. If you don't get some rest, you're going to get worse, and then you'll beg me to help you with your case, and begging isn't pretty."

"Fine," he said. He tapped his thigh, and Wojo raised his head. Tex held out his hand, and Wojo jumped down from the sofa, sniffed his fingertips, and trotted up the stairs by Tex's feet. Rocky raised his head, too, and watched Wojo and Tex leave the room. He turned his furry head toward me as if hoping for permission to join.

"Not tonight, Rocky."

He dropped his head, and his body followed. He stayed in that position while I cleaned up the kitchen, putting soup in Tupperware and letting it out to cool before putting in the refrigerator for Tex to eat tomorrow.

I started the dishwasher and straightened up the living room. We'd left things as they were while the Dallas police officers walked through, but now that they were gone, there was no point in letting Tex wake up to a mess.

I heard Tex's feet over my head, and then the creaking of the bed springs, and then nothing. How was he going to tell the people of Lakewood what he'd found? This case required a press conference so the news had something to report. Tex could suppress what he knew only for so long.

I sat on the sofa and stroked Rocky's fur while trying to make sense of a bucket of mismatched information. It came down to one thing. Two bodies were left behind in the woods for anyone to find: Yasmine Garcia and Winston Burr.

These were two people of wildly varying backgrounds. Yasmine was a police officer's wife, the mother of two who had become dissatisfied with the responsibilities of being a wife and mother and started working at a flower shop. Winston was a wealthy developer and philanthropist who kept the city of Dallas running with donations and expansion. They didn't have anything in common, but they were both dead at the hands of a murderer who seemed to have thought of everything. This wasn't a Doris Day movie. This was *Little Shop of Horrors*.

29

I woke on Tex's sofa with a crick in my neck and Rocky curled into my side. It was a little after six, and the townhouse was dark. I got up and stretched, went upstairs to check on Tex, and found both him and Wojo sound asleep. I went back downstairs and left him a note, then packed up Rocky and took off for the pool.

My mind was racing with information—or the possibility of getting it. I worked off most of my anxious energy in the water.

It was seven-thirty by the time I finished my swim. I showered and dressed in an outfit I'd packed in the go bag in my trunk. It was from the estate of Carol Kelly, manager of the Texas Book Depository from 1963 to 1970. While no specifics of her job could be found amongst her personal belongings, I pictured her working alongside of Lee Harvey Oswald, perhaps joining him for a cup of coffee on break or reprimanding him for being tardy. The stories that woman could have told . . .

Carol's wardrobe consisted of smart linen skirt suits hemmed to a modest length that each came with a matching top that had probably never been worn with anything else. All three pieces of each ensemble were hung on one hanger, as if having to mix and match each morning was not worth the effort. Sometime in the eighties, after she'd left the Book Depository for a job in the admission office of a local college, she'd taken to attaching Polaroids of coordinating jewelry and shoes to the hanger, simplifying the process even more.

Today's ensemble was a yellow skirt suit with a yellow-and-white-striped top. Honoring Carol's talent for coordination, I added yellow Keds sneakers and a white wicker handbag. Not only did I feel put together, I felt efficient as well.

I had a couple of hours to kill before picking up the funeral wreath from By George, so I drove to my studio and parked in the back. The sheet of plywood that I put in place after the vandalism was still there. I set Rocky up in my office with fresh water, food, and his favorite rope bone and made my first phone call. It wasn't lost on me that the person I turned to was Hudson, not Tex, but something he'd said was relevant to my circumstances.

After four and a half rings, Hudson answered in a voice laced with sleep.

"Hudson, it's Madison."

I heard rustling and some mumbled words, and then "Hold on." Seconds later, he cleared his throat. "Hey," he said, his voice low and gravelly. "Give me a sec." It sounded like he was being quiet so as not to wake the neighbors.

Hudson had always been a morning person like me, and shortly after we started working together, we'd determined that morning calls were more productive than evening ones, yet I couldn't help feeling self-conscious over the inappropriateness of the hour.

"Hey," he said again.

"Thank you for fixing the funeral home's air conditioning unit," I said. "I hope that wasn't too much to ask. They said you gave them a list of contacts."

"I didn't mind doing the job, but they need somebody who's local."

"Sure, that makes sense. I'm sorry I missed you."

"It's cool. Their return duct was disconnected. Like you said, it was easy money." He paused. "Was there a problem with it?"

"No," I said. "Not with that." Instead of spending time on pleasantries, I charged ahead. "You mentioned movie people here in Dallas. Something about the second unit director and a film crew?"

"That's right."

"Are they still here?"

"Yes."

"Do you have a way to get in touch with whoever's in charge?" I asked. Hudson was quiet for a moment longer than was normal, and I quickly allayed his fears. "This isn't about the movie," I said. "There was a break-in at Tex's townhouse last night, and a case file was stolen. It's a long shot, but I thought it was possible that the film crew saw something. Maybe someone was there in the neighborhood."

"At Tex's?"

"Yes."

Hudson coughed. I heard a click and then another sound that took me a moment to place. The sliding door at the back of his house. I pictured him letting himself out and closing the door behind him so his antisocial black cat, Mortiboy, couldn't escape. He spoke again, this time his voice at a normal decibel.

"The assistant director is a woman."

I held my breath in anticipation. Hudson knew something.

He'd seen it, or he knew about it. The film crew had told him something that he'd tried to keep to himself because he hadn't wanted to get involved. But Hudson was a good guy. He couldn't not help.

"Hold on, let me grab a pen." I reached into my cupholder and pulled a blank sheet of paper out of the printer tray.

"Madison, wait," he said. "There's a reason you didn't see me yesterday. There's something I've been meaning to tell you."

The sharp tone of Hudson's voice was different than any conversation we'd had before. I set the pen down. Hudson wasn't about to give me information—at least not the kind I wanted. "The second unit director is a woman. Her name is Jules. We've been—we're engaged." He paused for a moment. "I wanted to tell you the other day when I came by your showroom, but with the vandalism, the timing didn't feel right."

"And yesterday?"

"You have a file filled with handymen. I don't know why you called me, but on the off chance you wanted to drum up something from the past, I wasn't ready for it. Truth is I sat in my truck across the street from the funeral home for half an hour trying to figure out the best way to back out of the job."

"You saw me leave. That's why I didn't see you."

"Seems silly."

"No, it doesn't." I stared at the desk Hudson had built me, and then turned around and leaned against it. "I'm happy for you," I said. It was the right thing to say, and in time I knew I'd believe it. But right now, the surprise of it stung.

"Thank you," he said quietly. "The thing is, she knows about you. About us. About Tex. She knows the whole story because of the movie."

"It's ancient history, Hudson."

"I don't want you talking to her about a case," he said abruptly. "I don't want you talking to her about anything. Your life is with him, and that puts you in constant danger. She's different. She's great. She's creative and reliable and insightful, and at the end of the day, she wants to come home and hang out with me and Mortiboy."

I closed my eyes and stood still. "Mortiboy likes her?"

"He's curled up by her feet on the bed right now."

I'd always known that one day Hudson would move on, and any residual guilt over how things had ended dissipated. "I won't pull her into this," I promised.

Hudson was quiet for a moment. "If it's any consolation, there's no reason for the film crew to be watching Tex's townhouse. Nothing about the Pillow Stalkings happened there. I'm sorry, Madison, but even if I didn't ask you to give her some space, they wouldn't be any help."

I wished Hudson good luck and hung up. Rocky pawed at the inside of the door, and I knew what that meant. I clipped on his leash, and we went out back, where he huddled over a patch of grass near the trash. I collected his poop in a plastic bag and tossed it, then, on a whim, walked down the alley, around the block to Greenville Avenue. It was filling with the traffic of morning commuters going into and out of downtown Dallas. I stood with Rocky and watched the cars zip past.

Across the street, Bianca rolled a trash bin to the corner of the parking lot and waved. I waved back. She left the bin in place and jogged across the street between traffic.

"I was wondering how long it would take before you had your window fixed," she said.

"You'll have to wonder a bit more. I haven't heard from the insurance company yet."

"What about the lawsuit?"

I shrugged. "It's at a standstill."

"I asked my staff if they saw anything, but nobody spoke up. I can't say I'm surprised. After being questioned last week about the fight, they want to go about their business and not get involved."

"What fight?" I asked. At her confused expression, I clarified. "You said your staff was questioned about a fight last week. What was that about?"

"A family came in for dinner. From the second they walked in, I could tell the parents were at odds. I think they were trying to get through their meal because of their boys, but at one point, he raised his voice, and she yelled back. It escalated pretty quickly, and I asked them to leave."

"Did you call the police?"

"What was the point? One of them was a cop, and we all know the cops protect their own."

3 0

Nasty had said something about a public argument at a restaurant on Greenville, and I'd been so wrapped up in my problems that I hadn't stopped to consider who'd seen what.

"The Garcia family," I said.

Bianca nodded.

"I heard there were four witnesses who saw the fight."

"A customer who picked up takeout called the police from the parking lot. They came and questioned my staff. I told them to cooperate and tell the police what they saw, but I suspect they weren't forthcoming with information. Yasmine Garcia has been in here before. They feel like they know her."

"She dined alone? Or with someone else?"

"She always came with her boys." Bianca stepped back and studied me for a moment. "I thought you wanted to know about the attack on your store."

"I did. I do. But this—"

"You're asking for your policeman friend, aren't you?" Her

expression changed to one less friendly. "I thought I was talking to a neighbor, not a spy."

"Bianca, it's not like that. I know Officer Garcia. His wife was —" I caught myself at the last minute. I didn't know when Tex would be revealing what he knew to the public. I knew about Yasmine's fate because of privileged information. "Yasmine Garcia is missing. If you or your staff saw her in here, you might know something about where she is."

"She's probably as far away from her husband as she can get until a restraining order comes through," she said. "Not that that's likely. Yasmine Garcia is a regular customer. The police order a taquito platter once a year." She pointed to the plywood covering my front window. "And if *you* can't get protection after all you've done for the cops, then none of us can." She turned around and walked away.

When Tex had brought up keeping our relationship quiet, he'd framed it from the position of the police. It wasn't like he wasn't entitled to a personal life, but that one with a high-profile decorator who dressed like an extra from a Doris Day movie would be an invitation for scrutiny. I didn't argue with him over it because keeping things secret benefitted me as well.

But without coming out of the closet, I was faced with the reality of being his girlfriend. Bianca, who was something between an acquaintance and a friend, made it clear she didn't trust the police. Nasty had hinted at this as well. When the city cut the police budget, the police turned to the private sector to raise money. At that point, less affluent residents gave in to their distrust. No matter what my life looked like, by association, I was getting lumped in with the elite, and that put me at odds with the people I once called peers.

I stared across the street at Mad for Mod. Boarded up and

closed for business. Nobody cared that the one thing I wanted to do was off the table. Heat built up inside me. It morphed into anger, which shifted into rage. I'd been patient. I'd been cooperative. I'd closed my doors and filed my claim and gave Tex space, and for what? I was an island. A lone operator. There's no country for old decorators.

I wasn't comfortable leaving Rocky alone at the studio, not after the vandalism, so I took him downtown with me to pick up the funeral wreath from By George. George was offsite and had left the invoice with her assistant. The self-conscious side of me wondered if that were true, or if she were distancing herself from me as well.

The wreath was larger than I expected. After moving a bundle of vintage curtains from my trunk to the back seat, I laid it flat and slammed the trunk shut.

As alone as I felt, I couldn't help noting that my situation was the tip of the iceberg compared to Officer Garcia. From what Tex told me, Yasmine had been threatening to leave her husband long before she did, though whether Officer Garcia had been prepared for it was still in question. He'd traded a full-time job for full-time responsibility of two boys under ten. If given the choice, I'd see policework as the less stressful option.

The Garcias lived in a modest two-bedroom split-level house in Linwood Park. I knew this because I'd helped Tex send holiday cards this past December, and the address file was in my email inbox. Tex's requests that I not get involved might be valid, but being human was valid too. I picked up four gallons of ice cream from the local grocery store, plugged the address into my GPS, and arrived for a surprise visit. A trash truck was slowly moving through the neighborhood, making my choice between driveway or parking out front easy.

I looped Rocky's leash around my wrist and carried the bag of ice cream to the front door, which opened before I had a chance to knock. Officer Garcia, dressed in a Lakewood Police Department T-shirt and cargo shorts, greeted me.

"Ms. Night," he said. "Did the captain send you?"

For as long as I'd known him, Officer Garcia maintained the respect toward me that the police required of their officers. Other officers had taken to calling me Madison when Tex wasn't within earshot. I would have told Garcia to call me Madison, except in this case his behavior illustrated his ongoing commitment to following the rules of his job, and I didn't want to allow for the possibility that he was soon to be unemployed.

"No. I heard the news, and I wanted to offer my condolences. I can't say I know what your life is like right now, but I figured with two boys under ten, the chances of you needing ice cream were good." I held out the grocery store bag.

Garcia looked inside. "You got moose tracks."

"It was a gamble."

"It's my favorite flavor." He turned and went into the house. When I didn't immediately follow, he stopped and turned back. "Come on in," he said.

You could tell a lot about a person from how they lived. The Garcia residence was a study in southwest style. It wasn't my favorite trend, but I appreciated the combination of earthiness and textiles mixed with soft shades of coral and turquoise. A throw blanket made of brightly colored knit squares patched together with black yarn lay unevenly across the back of the sofa. Scattered around the floor were two and a half pairs of sneakers and a purple football. Rocky stuck his nose in a sneaker.

"Can I get you something to drink? We have Jarritos and coffee."

"What flavor Jarritos?"

Garcia looked surprised. "Lime."

The two boys ran through the living room to the kitchen. Rocky hopped up and barked. The taller of the two reached up and opened the refrigerator and pulled out two bottles of neon-green soda. He used a bottle opener to uncap them and handed one to his little brother.

"Dad? Can we play with the dog?"

"Ask Ms. Night," Garcia said.

"Can we play with your dog?" the younger boy asked.

"Sure," I said. I bent down and unclipped the leash from Rocky's collar. The boys carried their soda bottles to the back door with Rocky on their heels.

"I'm partial to orange," I said to Garcia with a smile, "so I'll go with coffee."

Garcia filled two mugs with coffee and, already knowing how I took my coffee, added a dollop of milk to both. We carried our mugs to the dining room table, where we sat around a rectangular table with a blistered wooden top. I could fix that with a hand-held orbital sander, but now didn't seem the time to bring it up.

"How are you holding up?" I asked as we sipped our coffee.

Garcia didn't answer right away. I sensed it wasn't because he didn't have the words, but more likely because he did and was afraid to speak them out loud. I gave him the time he needed to decide.

"I miss her. I miss her presence. I miss waking up to the dent she left in the bed when she got up before me, and the smell of her shampoo when she walked through a room. I miss her tuna noodle casserole and the way she lit up when she watched *Maid in Manhattan*. That was her favorite movie," he added sheepishly.

"I know it's difficult now, but it will get easier. You'll always have those memories of her, but in time, you won't miss her so much."

"That's what bothers me the most. I miss all these little things about her, but I don't miss her." He stared into his coffee mug, as if embarrassed to make eye contact after that admission. "Things haven't been good these last few months. All we do is fight. I'm afraid it's affecting the boys. My youngest is tentative. Shy. He's afraid to rock the boat. I hate that Yasmine is gone forever, but a part of me feels . . ." His voice trailed off.

I leaned forward, waiting for him to finish the sentence. What did he feel? Relief? Joy? Success? Power?

"Like the battle is over. Like I can breathe again."

He lifted his mug and swallowed several gulps, then stood and refilled it and returned. There was no way he'd finished his coffee in the amount of time it took me to take two sips, so I assumed he felt awkward about his confession and wanted an excuse to be out from under my direct attention.

"What can you tell me about your wife?" I asked. "What were her interests?"

"When we first started dating, she was bright and exciting. She had these big ideas about life. She loved living in Texas because she said every type of person lives in Texas. You had rich people and poor people of all different ethnicities. Self-made millionaires and worker bees. She used to say it was like a giant bowl of ceviche. Better because of all the ingredients, not because of one."

"How long have you two been married?"

"Seven years," he said. He quickly added, "Yasmine had a son before she met me, but I raised him like my own. I won't let anything happen to either one of those boys." He stared out the back window where the two of them sat in chairs, drinking neon-green soda from bottles, throwing a tennis ball for Rocky to retrieve, swinging legs that were too short to reach the ground. I felt his love for his boys emanating off him like a sonar pulse.

"Has Yasmine been acting differently?"

"There was something going on with her that she wouldn't tell me. It was little things here and there. I wasn't snooping, but I'm a cop. I notice things."

"Like what?"

"She started spending money more easily. At first, it was bottled water or name brand groceries. Then it was a throw blanket for the sofa, nicer toilet paper in our bathroom. The boys got new sneakers even though their old ones still fit. Nothing that I could complain about, because it was all for us, for them. But then my gun went off at that domestic dispute, and I got suspended. I told her we needed to tighten our belts for a little while."

"Did she understand?"

"She wasn't happy, but things went back to normal. And then she started getting flowers. She put them in a plastic water pitcher, but the next day, they were in a new crystal vase."

"How did she explain them?"

"She didn't. She said she didn't know who sent them, but I didn't believe her. I got mad and told her we were supposed to be a team and she needed to get with the program. That was it."

"What happened?"

"Yasmine said she never agreed to live like this, and if I didn't figure out a way to make her life more comfortable, she would. The next day, I came home to find two packed suitcases sitting by the front door. She wasn't home. I wanted to respect her privacy, but I couldn't help myself. I looked inside one of the suitcases and didn't recognize any of the clothes. I don't know where those things came from, but Yasmine never dressed like that. When she came home, I asked her to tell me what was going on. She accused me of spying on her, of trying to keep her under my thumb. She grabbed the suitcases and stormed out."

I wanted to ask Garcia if he knew she'd applied for a handgun, but that information had come from Tex. It was one thing to have an inquisitive, concerned-citizen conversation, but another to tip the hand of an investigation.

"Where were the boys?" I asked instead.

"Softball practice. It was my night to take the team out after, and it was too late to call one of the other parents to cancel out. We got pizza. When we got home, Yasmine was gone. Her phone was on the nightstand with a note that said, 'Don't bother calling.'"

"Do you think she left on her own?"

"I don't know what to think. I honestly thought she checked into a hotel to cool off. She's done that before, but usually for a night or two. This time, she was gone for two weeks. When Captain Allen called me, I was relieved—until he told me he needed me to ID her body."

I didn't know what to say after that. Silence stretched between us. There was one big question I hadn't asked, and as long as I was there, I had to inquire.

"After she left, did you find anything out of the ordinary? Any clues to where she might have gone?"

"No. Her clothes—the ones I recognized—are still in the closet. Her car is in the garage. If I hadn't seen the suitcases in the hallway before they went missing, I might have thought she was abducted by aliens."

I told Officer Garcia to call me if he needed anything, collected Rocky, and left. We walked down the driveway to my car. An empty recycling bin sat by the street, waiting to be brought back to the house. The lid hadn't been put on properly and rested a few feet away. Rainwater would fill the bin and make it impossible to move. I picked up the lid and carried it to the bin, glancing inside before snapping it into place.

I was wrong; the bin wasn't empty. Inside, plastered in place with rainwater and dirt, was a dying bouquet of midnight-blue roses.

I GOT INTO MY CAR AND CALLED THE POLICE STATION. "LAKEWOOD
Police Department," Imogene answered.

"This is Madison," I said. "Is Captain Allen available?"

"He's meeting with the police commissioner. Can I take a
message?"

"Have him call me as soon as he can."

"Why? Did you find a hot clue?" Her voice dropped low. "I bet
there's a secret lover. There's always a secret lover. Or a son who
came out of the woodwork. That's probably it—a son nobody
knew about looking for his inheritance. Or a daughter! Why does
it have to be a guy?"

Despite Tex's trust in Imogene, I knew better than to share my
newfound information with her. "Have the captain call me. It's
urgent." I gave her my cell phone number and hung up.

Tex was wrong about me making things more complicated.
I was the one person who could make things easy. And if he
were lucky, by the time his meeting was over, I'd have his
investigation back on track. My initial idea, the reason I'd

called Hudson about the film crew, wasn't a bust just yet. If I was right, then there was another person who might have been watching Tex's townhouse last night. I turned the corner and drove to the last place anyone would have expected to find me.

It was my second time at the Dallas Market Center in a matter of days. I parked close to the entrance and signed in at security. There were enough vendors supplying merchandise for Dallas's furry contingent that I wouldn't have a problem taking Rocky with me. I clipped a visitor badge to my yellow lapel, and Rocky and I walked to the elevator. He scored extra points by not stopping to sniff anything on the way.

We reached the second floor. Montgomery Design was stenciled on the window under a watercolor depiction of a pink-and-white ranch house. I made it to the doors and into the showroom before being spotted and recognized, both of which were small victories considering the security measures I'd had to follow.

"What are you doing here?" Brandon demanded. He picked up the receiver of his phone. I approached him with swift efficiency and disconnected his call.

"Calm down, Brandon. I'll make this quick. I know you hired someone to follow me, and I need his name."

"You're kidding me, right? I'm not giving you anything." Today Brandon was dressed in a white dress shirt with a red-and-blue-striped bowtie. He had on matching striped suspenders clipped to navy-blue trousers. His shoes were shiny black wingtips that he wore with no socks.

"This isn't about the lawsuit or the invasion of privacy. This is important." I held my ground while Rocky sniffed a set of shiny red plastic S-Chairs by Verner Panton. I'd always wanted a pair for my patio and considered inquiring about the price until I remembered Brandon was my sworn enemy.

"It's important? Oh, well then if it's important, that's different." He picked the phone receiver up again and pressed the star key. After a pause, he said, "Madison Night is creating a disturbance in my showroom right this minute. Yes, please. Thank you." He hung up and smiled at me.

"Today started out so boring. Who knew it would end with you being escorted out of the Dallas Market Center by security?" He rubbed the palms of his hands together like a magician gearing up to pull a rabbit out of a top hat. "My one regret is that I don't have popcorn."

Judging from how long it had taken me to get from the lobby to Brandon's showroom, I had about two minutes to talk. I didn't waste time on a comeback.

"Last night I was visiting the captain of the Lakewood Police Department."

"Business or pleasure? It had to be pleasure because you're under an injunction not to conduct business while the lawsuit is being reviewed."

My skin prickled. Until now, the cover story of me decorating Tex's spare bedroom had sufficed as a reason I kept going to his townhouse. But now, I was trapped. If I said I was working, I'd lose Mad for Mod. If I admitted we were dating, Tex's case would be compromised.

The whole reason I was here was to get a lead for Tex, and I couldn't blow that now. "Brandon, I was in the middle of a job for Captain Allen when you filed the lawsuit. The judge said I could complete any jobs in progress but not take on any new ones."

Brandon narrowed his eyes. "I don't remember the judge saying that."

In the hallway, I heard the bell announcing the elevator, and then the swoosh of the doors opening. Rocky, more easily distracted than I was, raised his head and trotted to the entrance of the showroom to investigate.

I balled up my fist around the leash. "Last night, someone broke into Captain Allen's townhouse. A case file was stolen. I assume if you've had someone following me, then they followed me there. Do with that information what you will, but I need to talk to your detective. He might have inadvertently gotten information that could catch the person who's trying to impede an open homicide investigation."

The color drained from Brandon's face as Nate Green, the flower designer, rounded the corner. Two security officers who looked barely out of high school followed. They were mid-twenties men, one short, compact, and fair, the other tall and dark with sloped shoulders and belly pooch. Nate's expression said he was ready for battle, but the security officers slowed up. They appeared to be unprepared to find a fifty-year-old woman in a yellow skirt suit as the disturbance with which they'd been tasked to deal.

"Are you okay?" Nate asked Brandon. "She didn't assault you, did she?" Nate put his hand on Brandon's back and comforted him.

"Mr. Montgomery?" the fair security officer asked. "Did you call for security?" He looked back and forth between Brandon, Nate, and me. I had to give Brandon credit. The expression on his face was one of fear. I wondered if he rehearsed it in the mirror in anticipation of this moment.

Brandon looked at Nate. "It's okay," he said. "I can handle this." He turned to the security team. "It's under control, guys. This was a misunderstanding."

I gave my best Doris Day smile to the men. The taller one seemed to interpret it as an invitation of sorts and grinned back. I dropped my smile slightly and crossed my arms. The men receded into the hallway.

"You should go too," Brandon said to Nate. "I'll tell you what happened when I get home tonight."

"Are you sure you'll be okay by yourself?" Nate asked.

"Oh, please," I said, rolling my eyes.

Nate followed the security officers down the hallway. Rocky, ever the loyal defender of my integrity, stood at the entrance to Montgomery HQ and stared at the men until the elevator doors closed.

"I assume you called off your guards because you came to your senses. Thank you," I said to Brandon. "Like I said, someone stole a case file from the police captain. Your detective might have a lead. If you'll give me his name, I'll leave." I waited for him to go on the offensive. Now that we were short three witnesses, he could verbally attack me all he wanted. He remained pale, and a drop of sweat appeared at his hairline.

"I can't. Those were the terms of the contract."

"Shouldn't he be more concerned about your confidentiality than you are about his?"

"Wait here." Brandon turned away and went into the stockroom. I knew better than to snoop, though the temptation was strong. When Brandon returned, he held a beat-up file folder that looked suspiciously familiar. He held it out to me. "That's the file from your boyfriend's townhouse." He dropped his head. "I took it on my way out."

"You?" I snatched the folder while it was being offered. "Why were you at Captain Allen's house? Why did you steal this?"

Brandon was clearly shaken up. "I heard you did a job there.

I've been watching the place. I thought I was going to catch you working, so I broke in and looked for evidence. When you came in, I went upstairs. I hid in the bedroom closet. Your boyfriend came home, and when you two went to the roof, I ran downstairs. I grabbed that"—he pointed at the file—"because I thought it was a client file. I wanted to nail you for taking business under the table."

"Did you look in here?" I tapped the folder.

He nodded. I didn't think it was possible for his face to lose more color, but his already-pale features turned a shade of green normally reserved for bundles of sage. "You weren't working on a decorating job."

"You have to tell the police about your detective."

"I can't."

"You have to. He might have seen something or know something. He can take this file back to the police, and you can keep me out of it."

"He's a she," Brandon said.

"Excuse me?"

"My detective. She's a woman. She owns a security company, and her contract calls for mutually binding confidentiality."

My skin prickled, and any remnants of the smile I'd given the security guards dissolved. "She didn't."

"Didn't what?"

"Brandon, who's your detective?"

He shoved his balled-up hands into the pockets of his trousers and hung his head. "Her name is Donna Nast."

3 2

I STORMED OUT OF BRANDON'S STUDIO SO FAST ROCKY COULD barely keep up. Just when I thought I could trust her, I thought. Of all the low-down, dirty tricks, I thought. Nasty deserved her nickname, I thought.

The warm rain was a stark contrast to the dry, air-conditioned temperature inside the Dallas Market Center, though I was so hot under the collar that the rain felt cool. I stormed to my car. I clicked Rocky into his dog safety harness and started the car. Nasty's phone was ringing before I put the car in reverse.

"What?" she answered.

"You took a job spying on me," I said. "How is that not a conflict of interest?"

There was a brief pause, and then, "A conflict with what? I don't work for you. I've never worked for you. There's a reason I didn't take your money." She paused for a moment. "I did tell you Brandon hired someone to follow you around. I gave you that courtesy."

"You're the someone!" I said. My voice was sharp and

accusatory, and Rocky, who recognized the tone from the moments when he peed on a carpet, hung his head in shame.

This was nuts. This was nuttier than nuts. This was worse than the time Tex stole my car and I reported it to the cops as grand theft auto.

I softened my voice for Rocky's sake. "You're the person Brandon hired to follow me around," I reiterated.

"Yes, I am. And you made my job considerably easier by calling me all the time. Did you ever wonder why I was always in your neighborhood?"

I hadn't. "I don't know how I feel about this."

"Let me tell you how you feel. You and Tex are trying to hide your relationship. If anybody else took the job, you'd both be outed. Tex would get pulled from the investigation for about ten different violations, and the media would have a field day with the fact that the police captain's girlfriend is being sued for fraud. Your legal problems will get knotted up in his case, and his politics will invade your privacy." She paused. "How'd you find out?"

"Brandon told me. I'm surprised you didn't know."

"I made him sign a confidentiality agreement. If he told you he hired me, then our contract is void."

It all made sense now. Brandon was scared of Nasty. More scared of her than of me or of Tex. Frankly, ever since she got pregnant I was a little scared of her too.

"He wanted you to spy on Tex's townhouse, and you told him to leave it alone," I surmised.

Nasty cursed. "He didn't leave it alone, did he?"

"He did not. He snuck inside and found a file on the counter. He thought it was a client file, and that he was going to catch me in a violation of the court order to cease business."

"What was in the file?"

"The medical examiner's notes on the two victims from the park. Autopsy reports, cause of death. Identity of the bodies."

"Where's this file now?"

"In my hand."

"I don't have to tell you to get that file directly to Tex but let me handle the Brandon part. If you want a future with Tex, you don't want to be the one to tell him your lawsuit might have cost him his case."

I WAS BURSTING at the seams with information for Tex. I gave Nasty half an hour to call him and tell him what had happened. There was no way the news of Brandon's actions hadn't reached him, and still, he hadn't called me back. I went to the precinct to turn over the file and be done with it.

Imogene was behind the desk, and Wojo sat next to her monitor. Tex stood in front. He straightened up when he saw me and Rocky. He tipped his head toward the hallway that led to his office and turned around, leaving me with the choice of following or walking out.

"I think he wants you to follow him," Imogene said in a conspiratorial whisper. "He's at the point in this case where nothing's going his way, so if I were you, I'd tread lightly."

Pettiness kept me from setting the file on the counter and leaving. A little curiosity, too. I wanted to hear how Nasty had spun things.

Tex was already seated behind his desk when I entered his office. I put my hand on the door to close it. "Leave it open," he said, "and sit."

I dropped into the seat opposite his desk and waited for further commands.

Tex stared at the folder on his desk. He picked up a pen and tapped the folder with the end of it. "We have a problem."

"I know. I talked to Officer Garcia this morning, and he said—"

"You did what?" He sat forward and slapped the palm of his hand against the surface of the desk.

"I went to see Officer Garcia—"

He cut me off again. "How do you know where he lives?"

"I never deleted your Christmas card list from my email. Do you want to hear this or not?"

"Not."

"But—"

He held up his hand. *"Not."* There was no ignoring Tex's reaction. He made it his superpower to read people while applying pressure. He set the pen down. "There's a lot of heat on you right now thanks to the lawsuit."

"Let me handle Brandon."

"This isn't about Brandon. I can't risk someone saying I jeopardized a case over a woman."

It was like Nasty had said: Tex was distancing himself from me. It felt a hundred times worse than my conversation with Hudson earlier that morning.

"This case requires all of my attention. That means no more picnics, no more sleepovers, and no more meetups at the pool."

"I understand the demands of your job, Captain Allen," I said.

I'd gotten in the habit of referring to him as Captain Allen when discussing him amongst others, but it was an old dynamic of ours, me calling him by his title to his face. It established a boundary between us defined by our jobs, not our compatibility. In the past when I'd said it, I'd wanted a reaction. This time too.

And I got it. As soon as the words "Captain Allen" were out of my mouth, Tex looked directly at me. His crystal-blue eyes bored into mine, and I felt a prickly sensation in my fingers and toes. My heart raced. I had an overwhelming urge to kiss him and an equally overwhelming one to slap his face. It was just like when we first met.

The electricity hung in the air for a long moment. Tex didn't look away. There was a gentle knock on the open door, and Imogene entered with a sheet of neon-green paper in her hand.

"Sorry to interrupt. Captain, you said you wanted to see the corrections before I made new copies."

Tex nodded, and Imogene set the paper on his desk. He flipped the paper over so the words were face-down, but not before I saw the details about the community watch meeting.

"I'm sorry," Tex said. "I know you want me to say it won't always be like this, but I can't."

I stood. "You should visit Garcia. Not because he's one of your officers, but because he's got midnight-blue rose petals stuck to the inside of his recycling bin. Maybe it means something, maybe it doesn't. I thought you should know."

I stormed out of his office. He didn't follow.

I was used to seeing officers at the front desk, but lately, it had been Tex and Imogene. Instead of having a core group of full-time cops, he now had a rotating staff of part-timers who clocked in and immediately went on patrol. Parking tickets, traffic violations, domestic disputes all were handled by cops redirected by dispatch to the site of the situation in question. More pressing cases demanded resources Tex didn't have.

Before exiting the building, I stopped by Imogene's desk to ask about her book.

"I'm stuck on a plot point," she said. "I don't want to be too predictable, but I also want to play fair with the reader." Behind her, the printer spat out colorful sheets of paper that filled the output tray.

"Do killers play fair?"

"It's an industry term," she said. "It means the reader should be able to solve the case with the clues I put in the book. No surprise information at the end."

"Yes, but sometimes unexpected things happen," I said, glancing back down the hall toward Tex's office.

"Not really," Imogene said. "They seem unexpected because you didn't see the clues. People are predictable. They want to control an outcome, so they orchestrate a situation. Good or bad, everybody's got a motive for how they behave."

"Is that what's happening with this case?"

"This one's a doozy. Every time I think I've figured out whodunit, I learn something new. It's been great for my work in progress." She tapped a notebook that sat next to her keyboard. *MURDER IN DALLAS* was written on the cover.

"You're not using case files for your story, are you?"

"I'll change the names to protect the innocent. Everybody does it." She stood from her chair and retrieved the stack of copies from the printer then set them on her desk.

I lowered my voice. "Can I have one of those?"

She picked up the flyers and moved them to the table behind her. "Sure," she said. She thrust a still-warm copy at me. "The meeting is at seven tonight. Maybe I'll see you there."

THERE WAS no doubt in my mind that Tex meant what he said. My nemesis having broken into his townhouse and stolen a case file was a serious problem. But I had serious problems too. These days, serious problems were my middle name.

Going home meant reporters, and I was less inclined to face the music today than before. I drove to my studio and parked around back. Without incoming jobs, Mad for Mod was little more than a storage space. I'd spent years accumulating items from estate sales, and my inventory was now overflowing. Brandon's lawsuit kept me from taking on new clients, but the vandalism had left me with a different agenda.

I walked Rocky to the dumpster and waited while he peed, then we went inside. He immediately went to his dog bed. I played my messages while sorting through the mail. The first two messages were hang-ups. The third was from the insurance company, requesting a callback. I ignored the rest of the messages and called the number.

"Hello, Ms. Night. This is Paul from the Kimble Insurance Group. How are you today?"

"I've been better, but if you're calling with news about the insurance payout, then I suppose my day will have turned around."

"I'm afraid your day isn't turning around," he said. His voice was upbeat to the point of being condescending.

"How long does an investigation of this nature take? It would be helpful to know when I can expect a resolution so I can make arrangements."

"Ms. Night, our investigation has revealed your involvement with an open police investigation and a relationship with the police. That raises questions we're not prepared to ignore."

I pushed my blond hair off my forehead and stood. "I don't

understand," I said. "How does my cooperation with the police have any bearing on your investigation? I've never even been a day late on my insurance premiums. Someone vandalized my showroom while it was closed. Valuable inventory items were damaged."

"Did this vandalism affect your ability to conduct business?"

"It certainly would have if I were open for business. The vandalism probably has to do with an open lawsuit against me."

"Yes, we discovered that information too. If the court rules against you in that case, you'll have to turn over everything to the defendant, correct?"

"Yes."

"Sacrificing inventory for an insurance check before there's a ruling by the courts could be seen as an attempt to manipulate the payout. A way for you to profit from your business before you lose it."

"That's not what's happening here," I said. "I'm the victim."

"That may be the case, Ms. Night, but until that case is settled, we won't know whether to cut the check out to you or to Montgomery Designs. There are too many questions about attention-seeking and misdirection for us to wrap this case up quickly. And a word of advice? Don't get too comfortable. These investigations tend to turn up details that business owners like yourself are trying to hide."

33

I DON'T REMEMBER HANGING UP THE PHONE. WITH THE INSURANCE agent's condescending tone ringing in my ear, I sank back into my chair and felt the particular numbness that accompanies hopelessness. Rocky, who'd always been intuitive when it came to my emotional needs, offered me his rope bone between his teeth. I tugged on one end, and instead of tugging back, he let go. A gift to cheer me up.

I picked him up and set him on my lap. He turned in a circle and then put his paws on my chest and nosed me.

"No matter what happens, we'll survive," I said to him.

He yipped twice in agreement. We cuddled together for a few minutes, and then Rocky grew restless. He hopped down and lapped some water and then looked up at me. I tossed his bone to him, and he set to work gnawing on it with intent. His focus was admirable. I guess that's why persistence is often likened to a dog with a bone.

The copy of the file on the By George job was where I'd left it after the vandalism. After Hudson had surprised me by showing up unexpectedly, I hadn't thought much more about the file. But now, with the insurance company all but accusing me of fraud, I circled back to the presence of paperwork that should have been in the hands of the legal team.

As I sat there, I heard sounds coming from the back. It wasn't trash day, and even if it were, there would have been no trash for the collectors to take. I left Rocky in my office and went to the door, where I spied Effie getting out of her Mini Cooper.

Five years ago, Effie Jones had looked like a typical college student. Long blond hair that was in a perpetual state of dishevelment, cozy sweatshirts and printed pajama bottoms that told the world she was too busy cramming for a final to think about real pants, and colorful Ugg boots lined in fleece regardless of the Dallas temperature. But since graduating college, she'd shed the PJs and Uggs and shifted into shrunken blazers over T-shirts and jeans—the business suit of the millennial CEO. She'd cut her hair into a shoulder-length bob, which, while still uncombed, was an immediate improvement.

After coming to work for me part-time, Effie had pushed me to update my inventory system, studied mid-century modern design in her spare time, and binged on the Doris Day movies I gifted her a few years ago. These days she was enrolled in business school. By mere proximity to her, I was getting the education I'd missed by starting the company on a wing and a prayer.

"Hey, boss!" she called out. She slammed her car door and approached me. As she got closer, she opened her arms and enclosed me in a hug.

I wasn't a hugger. Her gesture, though nice, felt awkward.

She patted me on the back. "It's going to be okay," she said. "Relax. Let go. Let the hug give you power."

If it were possible for me to go more rigid, I did. I leaned back and stared at her.

"It's hug therapy! We studied it in B-school. Did you know a lot of startups keep a professional hugger on staff? It's supposed to take away stress and make you feel less alone."

I stepped back. "I feel less alone now that you're here."

"Good!" She smiled. "Good," she said again, this time more relieved. "I don't know if I'm qualified to hug people professionally."

We went inside to get out of the hot sun, and Effie dropped down to the carpet to pet Rocky. The two of them had a reunion of sorts while I poured fresh water into tall pink Blendo glasses with faded gold rims; the discoloration was a sign of frequent use from a prior owner, and we felt it our duty to keep them in rotation.

"I got back from Mexico two days ago and saw that you called me," Effie said. "I called you back a bunch of times, but you never answered."

"Technically, Mad for Mod is still closed."

"I thought that might be the case. Did you have a chance to go over the file? Maybe find something to nail Brandon?"

"What file?"

"The file on By George. You got it, right? I put it on your desk before I left."

With everything going on, I'd forgotten all about the file I'd found sitting out the day the studio was vandalized. I remembered thinking he'd been behind the attack and wondering about whether Brandon had the capacity to go from legal action to physical violence.

"Effie, I thought we turned that documentation over to the lawyers?"

She shrugged. "I made a copy. You're good with the investigation stuff, and nobody else is going to care about this business as much as you do. I assumed you'd throw yourself into saving Mad for Mod like you throw yourself into solving a homicide."

Effie was right. There was no reason why I should have put my energy into helping Tex when I could have put it into saving my livelihood. I'd been acting like it was about to be ripped out from under the soles of my Keds, while my neglect turned it into a self-fulfilling prophecy.

"How'd you like to help me with the inventory?" I asked suddenly. "When this lawsuit is over, we're going to have to hit the ground running."

"Sure, boss!"

Effie's new inventory database was housed in the cloud. Her generation liked to think of themselves as disrupters, and it seemed the tried-and-true method I'd used to track my inventory was ripe for an upgrade. I'd ignored her suggestion at first but quickly came around. Specializing in a decorating style from seventy years prior didn't mean doing business that way, and despite my vintage wardrobe, I'd prided myself on running a twenty-first-century company.

Organizing my inventory had always been a diversion from whatever it was that was on my mind, and today was no different. I carried my laptop and keys out back to the storage locker and set up a satellite office. A few months ago, I'd come into possession of a sizeable stash of vintage posters from NASA, though they remained curled in plastic tubes that were conveniently lined up against a wall. I slung several of the canister straps over my shoulder and carried them inside where I could log them into the system. If I lost the company, it would be futile work. I suppose despite two rejections in a matter of hours, I was feeling optimistic.

We spent the next several hours unfurling posters, positioning them under glass, photographing them, uploading them into inventory, and adding metadata to make the database searchable, all while playing "Space Capades," an Ultra-Lounge CD compilation of atomic-era music. Whether I'd be hired to design a Martian man cave or Venusian she shed was a question for the future, but if that commission came my way, I would be ready.

Despite the oppressive temperatures, we plowed through the project until the last poster was entered into the database. Effie had found a bag of extension cords and ran them from inside the studio to outside, where they powered a row of small fans. In hundred-degree heat, even hot air feels better when in the form of a breeze.

It felt good to work. To accomplish a project the way I had in the days before Montgomery vs. Mad for Mod. When Doris Day was alive and living in Carmel-by-the-Sea, a mentor I'd never met, not the subject of countless interviews that left me feeling like I'd used her. Having Effie by my side reminded me what it was I was fighting for, and that I didn't want to lie down and play dead.

When we finished, I turned the CD player off and reached into my handbag for the neon-green flyer I'd taken from the police station. I spread the flyer out on my desk and called Nasty.

"What?" she answered.

"I'm going to ask you a favor, and you're going to say yes. That's non-negotiable."

"Sounds like somebody has some fight left in them."

"A community watch group has organized to discuss the

Garcia/Burr murders tonight. They're meeting at Alejandro's Restaurant near Greenville Avenue."

"Were you not listening to me earlier?" she asked. "You need to distance yourself from this case."

"I can't. The insurance company is withholding my check while they dig into my background, and if I try to hide anything, it'll look like I was lying."

"What do you want, Madison? Why am I the lucky person you called?"

"You're going to the meeting, right?"

"Yes," she said slowly.

"I need you to take me with you."

Effie, eager to spend some alone time with Rocky, agreed to dog-sit for a few hours. I left my recognizable car parked behind my studio and waited out front for Nasty. She didn't question my reasons for wanting her accompaniment. She also didn't seem thrilled to have a wingman.

We arrived at Alejandro's, a white-napkin Tex-Mex restaurant in an affluent neighborhood called Turtle Creek, a few minutes later. Nasty valeted her Saab, and we entered. I asked the hostess to direct me to the meeting while Nasty splintered off to the ladies' room.

"Right this way," the hostess said. She led me through the dining room to a pair of glass-paned doors. She eased one to the left, revealing four long dining tables covered in white clothes.

Baskets of homemade tortilla chips sat intermittently on the tables. People stood around the perimeter of the room, holding margarita glasses in varying stages of full to empty. A few turned my way, but most remained attentive to the conversations at hand.

Officer Clark stood behind a six-foot-long white table that held a box of donuts and a sign-in sheet. Last year, Clark had transferred from Tex's department to the Dallas Police Department. A high blood pressure diagnosis led him to change his diet and lose weight. The last time I'd seen him, it had been thirty pounds; the loose fit of his uniform indicated he'd gone on to lose more.

"Officer Clark," I said in an overly friendly voice. "I thought this was organized by the Lakewood Police Department. Did you transfer back?"

"Personal favor to Captain Allen."

I reached for the pen, and he moved the sign-in sheet out of my reach. "You know I can't let you in," he said.

"It's a community watch group. I'm part of the community. My studio was recently vandalized, and you know, I haven't noticed any additional patrol cars on my street. A community watch would be the perfect thing to help me feel like someone's looking out for my business."

"I'm under orders," he said. To his credit, he looked miserable about it.

"Can't you look the other way while I slip inside?"

"Whether you sign in or not, Captain Allen is going to find out you were here."

"She's with me," Nasty said, joining me by the table.

Clark, who'd been Nasty's partner when she was on the force, relaxed into the familiarity of someone whose company he enjoyed. He put his hands into the pockets of his uniform and shifted his stance so his feet were shoulder-width apart. I marveled at how Nasty's presence quickly brought out Clark's masculine side.

"You know there's no way he's going to believe that," he said. "Donna, you can go in. Ms. Night, you're out here with me."

I shook my head and pulled Nasty away from the table. "This isn't right," I said.

"Go with the flow, Madison." She left me standing with Clark and entered the private room.

"Want a donut?" he asked, offering me the box.

ONE HOUR, three bowls of free tortilla chips, and half a margarita for me later, Nasty exited the meeting. The drink was stronger than I'd expected, and the booze made me sluggish. I had switched to water about half an hour ago, which did little more than expand the overabundance of cornmeal in my stomach. One more in a series of not-great decisions.

I followed Nasty to the valet station. Her car was waiting for her. She handed the attendant a twenty and sat down behind the wheel. "Let's go," she said to me through the open window.

Nasty pulled the wheel hard left, and even with my seatbelt in place, I pressed up against the interior of the car. She drove back to Mad for Mod and pulled into a space next to my car. I'd refrained from asking her questions on the drive, assuming she'd tell me what she could when she was good and ready and not a moment before.

"Winston Burr was one of the ten richest men in Dallas. He owns seventeen hotel chains and puts a lot of money back into the local economy. Landing his account would be a game-changer for Big Bro Security."

I pointed to her baby bump. "The father of your unborn child is no chump either."

"Gerry and I have an arrangement. I don't want to muddy the waters by becoming one of his employees."

Nasty was either the brashest businesswoman I'd ever met or the most morally ambiguous, but since meeting her, I'd watched her redesign her life without consulting the Girl Boss handbook. She was driven and calculating and seemed intimidated by nothing.

"Tex knows more about this case than he told the press," Nasty said. "One of his victims was his biggest donor, and the other was the wife of his recently suspended desk sergeant turned officer."

"Turned stay-at-home dad," I added. "Winston Burr used his money to influence local politics, and that includes the police force. Men like him think they can get away with things other people don't, and that attitude might have gotten him killed. I don't know what Yasmine Garcia had to do with anything, but there's a good chance she was an innocent victim of a greedy man's corruption."

Nasty rested the palms of her hands on the steering wheel and then gripped the wheel tightly. I felt her anger and frustration. "You know, Madison, for all your vintage aesthetic, you never impressed me as the type of woman who doesn't like money."

"I like money as much as the next person. I don't think you can be in business for yourself and not like money."

"Then why are you letting the news tell you Winston was the target and Yasmine was innocent? They're making him out to be corrupt. In bed with the police. They're saying that because he donated money to law enforcement, they're in his pocket."

I held up my hand. "Tex's department isn't on the take. They're good cops, and they're understaffed, and they want to find out who committed this crime as much as anybody else does."

"Do you believe that?" Nasty asked. "Because there's a lot of people around town who would love to see the police bungle this investigation. The media is trying to make it appear as though the cops care about half of the residents of the city and not the half below the poverty line."

"You know that's not true."

"So do you. But it doesn't matter what we know. It's what they're telling their audience. How many people do you know who actively seek out news that offers an opposing point of view?"

She had a point. The world had increasingly turned into two factions: people who agreed with you and people who were on the other side. Long gone was an interest in dialogue or debate. It seemed that everybody cared more about being right than finding the truth.

"Why do you care about this so much?" I asked. "You're off the force, and you and Tex—"

"I don't do things for money, Madison. I have a moral code."

"I didn't say you didn't."

Nasty stared out the front window. After a couple of seconds, she cut the lights and turned off her engine. "This is confidential," she said.

"Of course."

"No. Not like 'don't tell your boyfriend I said this' confidential, but I-signed-a-contract confidential."

It seemed irresponsible, especially considering my lawsuit, for her to stand on the brink of breaking a contract that could have negative repercussions on her business. Nasty was smarter than that.

"Shira Burr hired me to poke around the murders. She knows Tex is caught between his friendship with her husband and his support of his officer, and she knows how easily the press could undermine the evidence. With Winston dead, his money goes to her, and she doesn't want to become public enemy number one."

"Do you trust her?" I asked. "That much money gives her a pretty good motive."

Nasty studied me. "Sometimes I forget you're not from Texas."

"Sometimes?"

She shook her head. "Shira comes from a long line of blue bloods. Her family's had money before Winston made his first real estate deal. It's one of the reasons they worked so well together. They were equals. What they had was real."

"So why worry about the money now? Can't she just let Tex do his job and trust the process?"

"If things were that easy, then sure. But we don't live in that world anymore. Controversy sells papers. How many reporters tried to interview you before the lawsuit?"

"One."

"How about now?"

"They're camped out on my lawn."

"That's right. Your Doris Day schtick got you a couple of clients, and your involvement in the local murder rate probably got you more. This lawsuit made you controversial. All that sweetness and innocence wrapped up in double-knit polyester is just hiding a no-talent hack who steals designs and rides other people's coattails."

I felt bile rising in my throat, a burning sensation that had more to do with Nasty's observation than the tortilla chips and margarita. "Is that what you think?" I asked in a tight voice.

"If that's what I thought, you wouldn't be in my car right now. But you know how mad that just made you? I can feel the heat coming off you in waves. Multiply that times fifty million, and you'll get close to what Shira Burr feels every time people say Winston bought the police or cheated the city."

"You think she's right to be angry," I said, and this time it wasn't a question.

"She gave me full access to their life: credit card statements, calendar apps, personal and professional contacts, the works. After some preliminary digging, it looks like the news has this one wrong."

"You have evidence to support that?"

"The way of the police is to identify the most obvious answer, and that usually comes from focusing on the victim. We have two victims here, and they're focused on Burr."

"That makes sense. He probably has a lot of enemies, and sorting through motives is going to take some time."

"Once the cops have a starting point, they zero in on suspects. People who saw the victim over the past twenty-four hours, people who had business with the victim. Personal squabbles, private affairs. Anything that could lead a person to a potentially deadly encounter, premeditated or not."

"I can't say I disagree with their method."

"I can't either. It's investigation 101, and ninety-nine times out of a hundred, it'll lead directly to the guilty party."

"And in the last one percent? What happens then?"

"That's when someone gets away with murder."

35

I DIDN'T WANT TO ADMIT IT YET, BUT I AGREED WITH NASTY. AFTER talking to Officer Garcia, I believed it even more. His wife had been mixed up in something that she'd kept from him, and it had gotten her killed. It was more likely that Winston was the innocent victim in all of this than Yasmine, but aside from an old yearbook photo that ran alongside a profile on Burr, the media treated her as a minor character in the double homicide.

"Tex won't talk to me about the case. He said he's getting a lot of pressure because of the money Burr gave the police force, and with the heat on me from the lawsuit, involving me would make things worse."

"Do you believe that?" Nasty asked.

"I don't not believe it."

Nasty pulled her car up to the side of my house and cut the engine. She turned to me. "Madison, you're off your game, and I don't think it's all connected to the lawsuit or the bodies from the park. I think you lost your footing when your idol died. I used to think your obsession with Doris Day was ridiculous, but everybody needs an anchor."

"Who's your anchor?" I asked.

"My mom. My sisters. Five Nasty women." She gave me a wry smile. "People have been calling us that long before I ever joined the force."

It surprised me to hear Nasty had family, and it surprised me even more to hear they played a role in her life. I hadn't expected to see this softer side of her, and I didn't completely trust that this wasn't a trap.

"Where are they?" I asked.

"Around. One sister lives in the panhandle, another moved to Shreveport. My parents live in Bluffview, near Love Field. We're all close enough to get together a couple times a year, far enough not to be in each other's business."

"It must be nice to have family."

"Where's yours?"

"They passed away."

I didn't bother explaining the effect their death had on me. I had neither siblings nor aunts and uncles. When my parents died unexpectedly in a car accident the night before my sophomore year midterms, my world changed.

After the expenses of their death and the debt left behind, the estate was insolvent. It didn't seem prudent to rack the debt back up by continuing my education, so I postponed it indefinitely. Instead of asking for my exams to be rescheduled, I took a job, which led to a career, a broken heart, and a move from Pennsylvania to Texas to start over.

These last few months of not decorating had made me realize the void that would be left in my life if life as I knew it was taken away. Everything and everybody I surrounded myself with had a connection to decorating.

"Madison, you're at a crossroads. Let the cops handle the case, and let the lawyers handle the lawsuit. The world doesn't need another pity party of one. It needs you to get back on your feet."

I thanked her for the ride and said goodnight. I went to Effie's apartment to pick up Rocky and then drove to Thelma Johnson's house. I was tired of not living my life. I didn't care if the lawn was covered in reporters; I was ready to answer any questions they asked if that would make them go away.

But the yard was empty. The attention span of the public only lasted so long, and the murders were far more salacious news than my fall from grace. Discarded coffee cups and unfamiliar food wrappers in my trash bin were the only signs that reporters had been there. Even the business cards that had been jammed into the doorframe had fallen and now lay wet and discolored on the concrete steps next to my sisal floor mat.

Instead of going directly inside, I sat on a two-seater swing that was partially rusted. A motion-sensitive light over the building next door switched on and cast a halo effect over the property and into my yard. Rocky, free from his leash, sniffed the weeds by the base of a gnarled oak tree in my yard. The tips of my sneakers connected to the ground, slowly moving the swing back and forth. Back and forth. Back and forth.

I'd been so full of pride that I hadn't stopped to consider that I might lose the case. That now it was more than a possibility. A tickle of anxiety spread through my arms and legs, brought me to the brink of tears, and made my lower lip quiver and my hands shake. It was guilt, not pride, spilling out from inside me. Whatever code existed within me, I'd violated it by not insisting on protocols or demanding a chance to present my concepts. I'd gone through the motions of a job that wasn't mine, and now I was paying for it with the most valuable thing I had.

I don't know if it was the darkness that enveloped my house or the glow cast over the property next door, or the innocence of a perpetually puppy-like Shih Tzu discovering a new corner of the yard he'd never sniffed before, but I felt something deep within me. It wasn't calming, but it also wasn't fear. It took me a moment to recognize the last time I'd felt this way, the night I'd decided to move to Texas. It was a night after a string of nights when I lay in a hospital bed while my knee recovered from a skiing injury and I saw how easy it would be to make a change.

It was the answer to my most oft-asked question: what would Doris Day do? She'd pick herself up, dust herself off, and start all over again. She had, more than once. So in her memory, I would too.

I dug my phone out of my handbag and redialed Nasty's number.

"What?" she answered.

This time I didn't mind her brevity. "You said you had a way to keep me from losing my business license. Is that still an option?"

"It is if you want it."

"I want it."

"Good. Welcome back, Madison."

I hung up, feeling lighter than I had in a month.

TWO DAYS of late nights and early mornings were taking their toll on me. I changed out of my yellow skirt suit and into a nightgown. It came from the estate of Mary Moon, the airplane parts factory worker who owned the coveralls I'd found while organizing the attic. Underneath a stack of coveralls that bore the logo for Bristol Jarvis airplane parts manufacturing was a flat milky-white box in near perfect condition. Inside was a white cotton voile nightgown trimmed with lace. Mary might have assembled airplane parts right alongside the men, but when she was relaxing at home, she appeared to have a taste for luxurious bedwear. The soft fabric felt nice against my skin, and after days of schlepping around in the rain, carrying breeze blocks, and working at the mortuary, I was in the mood to wear something feminine. I washed my face, slathered on moisturizer, and crawled into bed.

And then remembered the funeral wreath in the trunk of my car. Drat!

One professional failure was enough for the night. Two were unacceptable. I got back out of bed and pulled a man's checkered raincoat over my nightgown and boots onto my feet. I kissed Rocky and left for the funeral home.

36

I PARKED OUTSIDE THE BACK DOOR OF AKINS MORTUARY AND wrangled the funeral wreath inside. It was close to midnight, and turning on the lights would alert any passersby of my presence—which would in turn get questions from Edward or Arnold. I didn't want to admit to them that I'd let something important go unattended. Get in, get out, and get on with my life. Meme wisdom applied to a volunteer job.

I crept through the hallway toward the room where the memorial service was scheduled. Shadows from plaster pedestals cast onto the walls, making the place far creepier than it was during the day.

There it was again. Creepy. I hadn't expected to fall victim to the assumption that people who worked around the dead were wired differently than the rest of the world, but I couldn't shake the thought. There was something off about Arnold and Edward. Time spent with them felt incomplete, as if there was something happening behind the scenes that I wasn't being told.

I shook off the feeling. This was a family business, one that existed in almost every community across the country. People relied on funeral homes to treat their loved ones with respect. It was a job. Like any other job.

Once I was out of the rain, I carried the wreath directly to the climate-controlled closet so the blooms would remain fresh. I sealed the door upon completion of my task and headed back to the exit.

As I reached the memorial room, I peered inside. Someone had finished setting up the chairs. I approached the display of framed photos. Yasmine Garcia had been a pretty woman, with long, dark, straight hair, and a bright smile. Even in snapshots, I could see her spirit. From the clothes she wore, I categorized the pictures as work, vacation, and social. There were no photos to represent her family life.

So much had been published about Winston Burr. Philanthropist. Businessman. Husband. Father. Millionaire. But were the rumors right? Had Yasmine Garcia simply been in the wrong place at the wrong time? What was her role in all of this? Had she witnessed the murder and then gotten caught, being a loose end that confused the investigation by the lack of ties back to Winston?

I studied a small, blurry picture of Yasmine in a simple white shirt and black trousers. There was something familiar about the background, but I couldn't place what. Too many people were in the photo with her, a small cluster of folks smiling and holding drinks. Wherever they were, I felt like I'd been there too.

I became aware of a sound. There'd been no cars here, no indications that I wasn't alone. I tiptoed out of the memorial room to Arnold's office and switched on the security monitor. Outside the exit, Officer Garcia pulled a framed portrait from the back seat of his car. He carried it to the building, where he bent down and propped it against the door. He stepped back and stared at the image. The angle of the security camera was such that I could see him but not it. He looked up at the camera and squinted his eyes. He turned around and looked in the direction of the pavilion and then at the camera again.

What was he thinking? That whoever had killed his wife had been caught on camera? I already knew that wasn't the case. Tex's investigation exposed that the monitor wasn't hooked up to a recording device. It served as a window, a screening device for the person in the office to identify delivery people and potential customers.

Garcia seemed not to have been privy to Tex's findings. He pulled his phone out of his pocket and took pictures of the camera, and then shielded it and walked back to his car. I expected him to drive off, but he didn't. He climbed in, closed the door, and broke down. Even with the glare on the front windshield, I could see him hunched over, his shoulders shaking and his head leaning against the wheel.

My heart went out to him. I couldn't see him committing murder, not one, not two. I'd seen supposedly good people do bad things over and over. I'd been nearly duped by a few of them and had experienced some narrow escapes myself. But I couldn't believe the case the media was trying to spin. This man, who trained to become a peace officer, who cared for two young boys. This man who watched over Rocky and convinced Tex to adopt Wojciehowicz.

Garcia got out of his car a second time. He wiped his eyes and then looked at my car. My very recognizable blue Alfa Romeo parked two spaces away from his sedan.

If asked about this after the fact, I could pretend it had been left there overnight. I could invent a plausible excuse for having been here, maybe something that included me and Tex in separate cars and him giving me a ride home. Despite our attempts to keep things under the radar, I suspected Garcia had picked up on the shift in Tex's and my relationship. He *was* a police officer.

He put his hand on the hood of my car. At first, I thought he was using it for stability—silly me—no, he was more likely seeing if it was warm. And even with the rain, it had to be. Lying would be recognized for what it was: an untruth designed to hide my whereabouts.

What had Garcia left outside the door? Now that he knew I was here, would he reclaim it? What would his next move be?

He turned his back on my car, wiped his eyes, and approached the entrance. Again, he looked directly into the monitor. This time he knocked.

There was a part of me, the part that wanted to trust in the good in people, that believed Garcia was innocent. I'd interacted with him several times over the past months, and he'd been nothing but friendly. He couldn't have killed his wife and Winston Burr. Could he?

That was the thing. I'd been wrong in the past, and it had almost cost me my life.

I called Tex. "I'm at the mortuary. Officer Garcia showed up. He's outside. He recognized my car, and now he's waiting for me to open the door."

"Can you pretend you left your car there overnight?"

"He already felt the hood."

"That's what I would have done. Alright, Night, let him in."

"But I'm alone here. You always say—"

"I know what I say. Listen closely. The evidence I was waiting on from the lab came back, and I've got enough for a warrant. Garcia isn't the killer. I'm at the judge's house waiting on a signature right now. I can't risk this case not going by the book, so I can't say anything more than that. But Garcia's been cleared."

"Quinn? The air conditioning guy?"

"I've said all I can."

As much as I wanted to ask, I knew Tex was taking a huge risk by telling me what he had. I thanked him and hung up and went to the door. Garcia had turned away, and whatever the large rectangle was that he'd propped up against the door was now being carried back to his car.

I opened the door. A sheet of rain fell, coating the night in a wet gray filter. "Officer Garcia," I said.

The stocky police officer turned toward me. "Ms. Night." He pretended not to notice my raincoat, nightgown, and rain boots, but did a poor job.

I retreated from the entrance and held the door open. "Don't stand there in the rain. Come inside."

He followed me down the hallway. I didn't feel comfortable using Arnold's office, not with an unexpected after-hours visitor, and aside from the foyer, the other room was the memorial hall. Garcia made the decision for us, noticing the setup of the room from the hallway. He went inside, set his package on the front row of cane-backed chairs, and stared at the display of his wife.

"I promised her I'd be there for her. I'd help her take care of the kids, and no matter what, our family would come before my job. I said I wouldn't leave her alone to care for them. I should have made her make the same promise back to me." He started to cry again.

"You'll be okay," I said. "Your boys will be too."

Garcia looked at me, his eyes bloodshot and puffy. "It's all my fault. When I got suspended, I couldn't provide. Yasmine wasn't supposed to have to work, but she did. If my gun hadn't discharged at that domestic violence call, she'd still be alive."

"No," I said quickly. I put my arm around his shoulders to comfort him. He seemed not to notice my awkwardness and turned his face into my shoulder. I felt his body shake with the jagged breaths that accompany suppressed tears.

After a minute of silence, he pulled away from me. "When the newspaper contacted me about a photo to run with the story, I was angry. People didn't care about Yasmine. Winston Burr was the story. The reporter said they thought it would be a nice touch to add an inset photo of her with the article. She was an afterthought to this whole city."

I'd wondered why the news outlets went with a yearbook photo, pulled from public records, instead of a more recent picture. Now I understood.

"She wasn't an afterthought," I said. "She was a mother to your boys. She was respected at their school, and she was respected by the other police officers. I've seen the two of you at events. Don't let one reporter's mistake influence the way you remember her."

Garcia picked up the wrapped rectangle and unknotted the twine around the butcher paper. Raindrops had marred the wrapping, leaving behind misshapen blobs of wetness. The twine came off, and the paper fell to the ground, revealing an enlarged photo of Yasmine Garcia dressed modestly in a white sweater and black skirt. She stood in front of a split-level house in the suburbs. Two boys dressed in similar attire, white shirts and black trousers, stood on either side of her. Their hair had been slicked into place, unnaturally for eight- and ten-year-old boys. One of them looked up at her, and the other pointed to something out of frame. Yasmine stared straight at the camera with a broad smile on her face.

"We wanted a family photo," Garcia said. "I was about to set the timer and join them, and an ice cream truck drove by. Marco pointed to it, and Luis started begging to postpone the photo and get ice cream instead. It was a typical day with two boys who can't stand still for five minutes, but instead of getting mad at them, Yasmine stood there and smiled. She said things were going to be okay, and I believed her. That was two months ago."

"Officer, you said someone sent your wife flowers, and she wouldn't say who. What were they?"

Garcia shrugged. "Midnight-blue roses. The boys thought they were cool, so I kept them until the petals turned. I threw them out a few days ago."

I took the framed image from Garcia and carried it to the front of the room, where I set it on the empty easel. I backed away. The rest of Dallas might be mourning the loss of a philanthropist, but in this room, the loss was all about Garcia's wife.

The longer we stayed in the room, the harder it was to think of a reason to leave. I couldn't remain there all night, and I couldn't let Garcia either.

"It's late, and the memorial service is tomorrow. I need to lock the place up." My heart broke over the look on his face. "Why don't you wait here while I get my things? We can walk out together."

He nodded. I smiled and left the room, pausing by the door to turn around and watch him by the table of photos.

I still didn't know what events had led to the double homicide. The news didn't seem to know either. A few reporters had floated the idea that the deaths weren't connected, though the similar condition of the bodies indicated otherwise. The police were holding onto that detail, so the public didn't know what I knew.

As I walked down the hallway, I became aware of an unpleasant smell. The more I tried to ignore it, the worse it got. I pulled my shirt up over my nose, but the rank odor got into the back of my throat, and I coughed. It was getting worse.

I entered Edward's office. Unlike his son's, Edward kept his desk neat. Paperwork had been either filed or clipped and placed in a wooden tray behind his chair. A generic watercolor of a fishing boat hung on the wall behind his desk, and an assortment of fish magnets decorated the side of his metal file cabinet. Other than those, the office showed little personality.

The offending smell got stronger the farther inside I went. Behind the desk, I spotted a partially open take-out container jutting from of the trash. Refried beans had oozed out and dripped onto the items beneath it.

No wonder it smelled in here. It had been sitting in that trash can since yesterday, and with the broken A/C unit, this discarded food had had time to stew. By tomorrow's service, the smell would become unbearable. It had to be removed tonight, far enough that it wouldn't offend.

I lifted the bulging trash bag out of the bin. The contents strained against the cheap plastic. The last thing I wanted was for the bag to break. I set it back in the trash bin and carried the whole thing to the back exit. The dumpster was behind the property, and I expected to be in and out before Garcia noticed I was missing.

A padlock was fed through the hatch on the dumpster. I circled the unit, looking for a side access panel, and found a laminated sheet of instructions taped to the outside. Trash pickup dates were marked, as was a reminder that because services were scheduled for Saturdays, no trash was to be placed inside the bins on Fridays.

Just my luck. I went back to the door and tried to open it. It had locked behind me. I pounded on the door and then slapped it with my open palm, but the door was solid steel, and I doubted Garcia could hear me over the rain.

The nearest trash bins were on the other side of the fence by the pavilion. I hadn't intended to leave Garcia alone inside for long. I hurried to the nearest public trash container and pulled the plastic bag out of the bin. The plastic split before I could get it into the trash can, and the smelly contents spilled onto the ground.

Something under the take-out container caught my attention. It was a thick catalog of sorts. With the toe of my sneaker, I moved the container out of the way and exposed the cover of the Farmer's Almanac. It was from this year. Colorful neon Post-its jutted out from the pages. Rain pelted both me and the mess. The food would be picked over by wild critters or washed away by morning, but the book would be ruined. I kicked it out of the way of the food and then picked it up and carried it to a dry table under the pavilion.

I'd seen the almanac on Arnold's desk the first day I was at the mortuary. I hadn't thought much about it. It was an essential tool in their planning process. It couldn't accurately predict the weather, but it was the closest thing they had to a crystal ball.

So why had it been tossed? I flipped to the first bookmarked page. Notes inside had been taken about a burial service: name and date. Same for the second bookmark. The dates were months ago and the bookmarks sporadic; for the first time, it hit me that Akins Mortuary was painfully underutilized for funereal services.

The rain around me picked up. I thumbed through the pages of the almanac while waiting for it to cease. I reached the week prior to when the bodies were found in the trash bins and stared at an unexpected item that was pressed between the pages.

A midnight-blue rose petal.

3 8

BLUE ROSE PETALS HAD BEEN ALL OVER THIS CASE, AND I STILL didn't understand what they meant. The unusual shade seemed to indicate artifice, not exclusivity. One florist said he didn't work with dyed flowers, and another had shrugged off the request like it was no big deal. There'd been discarded blue roses in the recycle bin outside the Garcia residence, and a couple dozen stems scattered on the counter of Akins Flower Shop, a bouquet-in-progress, the day I'd discovered the crime scene. If roses were the clue that tied everything together, then what did the petals lead to? And why were they all over this case? For this clean a crime scene, why had the killer been so lazy when it came to this detail?

I ran my thumb and forefinger over the sueded texture of the petal. Traces of blue transferred to my fingers. I let the petal fall and turned my attention to the almanac. Notes had been made on the page and in the margin. The prediction of rain and the expected duration of the storm. A map of White Rock Lake that had been marked up with the location of the public trash bins. A timetable of when the sun went down and when the lights went on.

I had an uneasy feeling that this almanac hadn't ended up in the trash by accident. It was directly tied to the window of time when Winston and Yasmine's bodies had been discovered.

I'd wondered about the rain. About the convenience of the bodies being discarded right before a rainstorm washed away evidence and kept people from frequenting the park. Nobody could have known it was going to rain, I'd said. But somebody could have. Somebody like Edward Akins.

Edward Akins? That nice, befuddled old man who wanted to spend his days fishing?

But what if he secretly harbored a grudge against Winston, if he never got over the fact that his childhood friend had grown up to become a millionaire and now owned the one thing he'd built? Arnold said they'd been friends once, but his dad didn't talk about their falling out. The sale of the mortuary to Winston kept the Akins family name in place and the Akinses employed. Arnold called it a win-win. But what if Edward hadn't shared his true feelings with his son?

I imagined how the crime might have played out. Edward killing Winston at the nursery—how? Hit him over the head with a gardening spade? And then what? He wanted to eliminate any witnesses and did Yasmine in too?

I tried to picture the old man committing the crimes and disposing of the bodies. It seemed ridiculous. I doubted he could do it himself. Did that mean he had help? Quinn? Arnold? Was this a family affair? Arnold wasn't interested in the funeral business, and his dad wanted to retire. I couldn't believe they'd go to all this trouble to protect something they seemed okay with giving up.

Tex had said he was waiting on a signed arrest warrant. He already knew who the killer was. He was following protocol to the letter, but he hadn't ordered me to leave. Would it have hurt his case if he did? Our relationship was still secret. If he cautioned me to get out of there, he'd tip his hand on knowledge of evidence before his case was closed, and in a court of law, that could cost him.

Until now, tonight, this moment, I hadn't truly felt what it was like to date a cop. It was one thing for Tex to warn me to stay out of his investigations when I was simply a public nuisance, but now that things were personal, a whole new batch of concerns were introduced to the mix.

He wasn't keeping our relationship secret because he was embarrassed by me. He was keeping it secret to protect what we had from what it would be used for when it became known.

As smelly as the almanac was, it was evidence. I could take it back to the funeral home and have Garcia give it to Tex. He could be the one to find it, not me.

The problem with that scenario was the trash. I couldn't explain Garcia finding the almanac if the trash wasn't there to be found too. There had to be a reason for him to go into Edward's office and go through the trash—and the answer was the partially rotting days-old food.

I went back to where the trash bag had split and used the trashcan to scoop the now-wet contents back into the bin. On some level, I knew my efforts were futile. The wet bin, the rain-soaked contents, the mud that now coated the trash. Regardless of how innocent the discovery of the clue in the trash was, what I was planning to do was evidence-tampering, plain and simple.

I'd gotten so lost in my thoughts that my grip loosened on the almanac, and it fell into the mud. Splatters kicked up onto the toes of my rainboots and the hem of my nightgown. I picked up the book, and a sheet of paper fell out. I snatched it before the rainwater could distort the information on the page, and what I saw sent a chill straight through me. Winston *had* bought out the flower shop, but he didn't leave it in his name. And a whole different story appeared in my head, one with a more solid plot. Not a story of transactional business, but one of jealousy and love and greed.

I needed to get Garcia. I dumped the trash on the ground and turned back to the mortuary.

"Where are you going?" asked a female voice.

I turned to confirm the identity of the new property owner for Akins Flowers: Shira Burr. The rubber sole of my boot shot out from under me, and I landed on my butt in the mud. Splatters of dirt covered the torso of my nightgown. I put my hands on the ground to give me leverage to stand, but the ground was too slick. I turned myself over onto my hands and knees and then slowly placed my feet underneath me until I was standing. I was so coated in mud and rotten food scraps that I didn't need a shower, I needed to be hosed down.

"You forgot this," Shira said. She held out the almanac in one hand and a gun in the other. Her hands were covered in thin black rubber gloves. She was dressed in black yoga pants and a black hoodie. A black knit hat was pulled down over her red hair, which had been knotted in the back. The harsh lines of her tattooed-on eyebrows seemed incongruous with her freshly-scrubbed face. "If the police don't find the evidence, they won't be able to convict the killer."

"How do you know that's evidence?" I asked.

"Trust me," she said. "The contents of that book will take care of all the loose ends."

I couldn't fathom what would bring the widow of a local millionaire to the site where his body was discovered unless she'd known I was there all along. The woman in front of me was either deep in the throes of grief or guilty, guilty, guilty. Her attire, taken directly from the how-to-be-anonymous handbook, indicted the latter.

"I'm sorry for your loss," I said, stalling for time. It was the same thing I'd said to Garcia that led to him breaking down in tears and telling me a story about his wife.

Shira scoffed. "Loss? I'm the richest woman in Dallas. And now I don't have to use my inheritance to pay off the women my husband sleeps with." She cast a quick glance at the trash bin closest to us. "Or the ones who snoop around our lives, looking for dirt."

"Yasmine Garcia didn't sleep with your husband. If her hands are dirty, it's because she works with plants."

"She delivered our flowers. I trusted her. She used her position in my house to blackmail me," she said.

"Blackmail you? *You* had an affair?"

Shira scoffed. "I'm not foolish enough to have an affair. The rules are different for rich men and their wives. Winnie had a wandering eye. I took care of them when he was done. I'm the one who made them disappear."

"You murdered them too?"

"It was far more pedantic than that. I bought them off. I've paid off every one of his women, and there have been a lot. Women all over this town are sporting Cartier watches and enjoying the perks of country club life thanks to me buying their silence. Protecting Winnie's reputation as a devoted husband has become a full-time job. My mother told me I'd have to do things I never expected to do if I married a man like Winston Burr, and she was right."

"I doubt your mother meant murder." My left foot slid in the mud, and I repositioned them for better stability.

Shira kept her gun trained on me. "Yasmine Garcia ruined everything. She was delivering flowers to the house and found the confidentiality agreements in my bedroom. She thought she could blackmail me. If she'd slept with him, I could have handled her too, but there was no way to contain her knowledge. She had to go." She spoke of double homicide with indifference. Like she'd overcooked a turkey.

We were feet apart, Shira armed with a gun and me armed with an almanac that smelled like refried beans. For a case that was covered in flowers, my situation stank.

And then I realized the flowers weren't the clue. The absence of flowers was the clue. Blue roses were all over this case, they were everywhere, except the empty vase at the Burr residence the day Tex and I arrived to give Shira the news. She'd claimed not to know Yasmine, but the flower deliveries would have connected them. I'd bet a hundred midnight-blue roses that if I asked Nasty to find flower delivery invoices in the cache of personal information Shira had given her to help solve the case, Nasty would come up with nothing.

"You killed her," I said. "You killed them both."

"I had to," Shira said. "She told Winnie on me. He didn't know I've been buying off women all over town. He accused me of turning him into a career path for wayward floozies. I was simply cleaning up his messes and keeping him free from lawsuits. I did him a favor, but he didn't see it that way."

"You can't do things for people who don't want your help and expect them to say thank you," I said.

"It was an act of generosity. I loved him. I protected him."

"By committing murder?"

"By fixing a problem," she said.

"How did you do it?"

"Winnie gave me the idea when he told me about the flower shop. The owners defaulted on their loan, and for the first time in our life together, I saw Winnie feel remorse. He actually suggested letting that old man keep the flower shop—something about being childhood friends and taking credit for catching a twenty-pound bass—" She rolled her eyes at the notion that anyone would brag about their catch of the day. "That's when I knew the flower shop was the perfect spot. No one would connect me to that location."

I barely heard her. I'd been ready to condemn Edward Akins over a secret, long-held rift between himself and Winston, and here the fight that broke up their friendship was over bragging rights to a fish. I was seriously off my game.

"You killed Yasmine Garcia at the flower shop," I said.

"I killed her and then asked Winnie to meet me so I could show him how I handled things. I thought he'd be thankful, but he called me ungrateful. He said he might have slept with other women, but he came home to me. As if that was enough."

Shira's eyes were red, shot through with visible capillaries that were engorged with blood. Strands of her normally styled red hair had escaped the chignon and curled out from under the bottom of her knit hat.

"And then you killed Winston too."

"It was never going to end. The women, the affairs, the payoffs. On and on and on. I couldn't avoid them. They started showing up at the club and the charity balls. One became Winnie's stylist.

Another was his handball coach. They were everywhere. Like cockroaches."

"You could have left him. You have family money."

"Who do you think bankrolled Winnie's early projects? Where do you think he got the money and the connections to enter Dallas society and be accepted as one of their own? I staked my family's reputation on him. Everything I had is tied up in properties and investments, and if Winnie's reputation is tarnished, mine goes with it."

"There were—there are—other choices. You always have choices."

"I wasn't born to be a working girl, Madison. This is my life. I'll do what I have to do to protect it." She readjusted the gun. Without spelling it out, she'd made it clear that I was one more threat to her lifestyle, and what was one more murder to her?

"A life you have to orchestrate isn't a life," I said. "It's a charade. When people scratch the surface, they're going to find the truth." As soon as I said the words, I knew the insurance agent had been right about secrets; eventually, truth will out.

"What's your price?" she asked. "You seem to care about that business of yours. God knows a normal person would have walked away after the vandalism."

"How do you—wait. You? *You* vandalized my showroom?"

"I knew how to handle the police. Yasmine Garcia gave me that much. But you? You're a do-gooder with too much time on her hands. I had to keep you busy."

"The insurance company thinks I was behind the attack. They think I'm trying to look like a victim because of this lawsuit."

Shira laughed. "I can make your lawsuit go away. I can set you up with jobs with the wealthiest members of Dallas society. I can put you on a six-figure salary as my decorator, and you won't have to work another day in your life. All you have to do is sign a confidentiality agreement and take that"—she gestured toward the soggy almanac with the gun—"back inside the mortuary so I can finish framing the old man for those two murders."

She made it sound so easy: take the money and keep my mouth shut. And as unbelievable as her frame job was, it was the same conclusion I had reached right before I found the bill of sale tucked between the pages.

This was the deal she'd offered women all over town. But what Shira Burr was asking wasn't easy. It didn't matter how much money she threw at me, or how many lawsuits she made go away. To sit with that information was to accept a death knell on my relationship with Tex. It would close the door on believing that bad guys got caught and that justice prevailed. What she asked of me was so foreign, it was like asking me to give up my vintage attire and dress like Lizzo.

Lightning flashed overhead, quickly followed by rolling thunder. Another series of rumbles followed, this time from the other side of the fence. As the sound grew closer, I placed it: the fluttery motor of the golf cart engine. It sounded like it was headed directly for us even though shrubbery and a metal fence stood between us.

The engine got louder. Suddenly, the tree line bent toward us, and the golf cart split through the fence. The impact stopped the cart, which sat off-balance on two wheels. The wheels on the raised side continued to spin. If there was a driver, he or she had been thrown from the seat.

Shira fired her gun at the golf cart. I searched for a weapon to defend myself against her and spotted the lid to the trash can. I grabbed the handle and crept toward her. She turned around, and I held the lid in front of me like a shield. I barely heard the click of her gun over the pounding of my heartbeat before a second shot rang out.

Shira screamed and dropped to the ground. I lowered the trash can lid. And Officer Garcia stood by the opening in the shrubbery with his gun trained on the woman who'd murdered his wife.

Officer Garcia was a hero.

When he discovered that I'd vanished from Akins Mortuary with the smelly bin of trash, he got suspicious. My car was still out front, and the wet carpet inside the back door indicated I'd left out the rear. The dumpster was locked, so he had no clear idea of where I'd gone or what I'd done.

The rain made it difficult for him to proceed on foot, so he took the golf cart. Garcia didn't know the brakes stuck, so what started out as a convenient way to cover the grounds turned into a joyride that was anything but. As he neared the tree line, he overheard Shira confess to murder. Whether he intended to stop or to call for backup was unclear. The faulty brakes made the decision for him, surprising Shira, redirecting her attention, and changing the outcome of what had seemed like an unwinnable situation for me.

Shira Burr wasn't dead. She'd been shot in the leg, causing her to land face-down in the mud. Garcia handcuffed her and called for an ambulance and assistance. There was no escaping a face-to-face with Tex.

It was a week later, and I'd barely seen Tex after giving my statement. If the press conferences, media interviews, autopsies, and Shira's hospital confession hadn't worn him out, the antihistamines did. I took it easy myself, relying on the local paper for updates in what had turned out to be an unlikely story about love, infidelity, justice, and flowers.

Shira's confession was announced the same day as her book deal. She received a seven-figure advance for a manuscript she'd write from jail. The money was earmarked for an account that maintained her estate. She wouldn't personally see a dime of it, though the knowledge that she'd earned millions from her story seemed to satisfy her in a way that coverups and murder had not.

As the papers reported it, Yasmine Garcia arranged for Shira to pay her off at the flower shop. Shira followed Yasmine to the nursery, confronted her, and killed her. When she called her husband to show him how she'd dealt with their problem, he got angry. She claimed his murder was self-defense, but I doubted a jury would believe her.

To hide the evidence, Shira stripped both bodies, hosed them down, and put them in separate trash bins. She used the lift attached to the flower delivery van to load the trash bins into the back and then transported them to the park. She hadn't needed to move the bodies into city-owned trash bins, only to leave the new trash bins behind. She'd timed the whole thing for the day after the city trash collectors emptied the bins by the park, so the bodies went undetected. To confuse investigators, she scratched up Winston and Yasmine's skin with thorny rose stems.

The rain kept picnickers away, and the planted flower petals, a unique color that Shira herself wouldn't be caught dead displaying in her house, served to connect the bodies back to the Akins family business.

At least that was what she'd hoped. As was the case with most people who thought they were smarter than the police, Shira's plan was full of holes. The rose petals she'd used as a clue to distract the police led back to Akins Flower Shop and identified the scene of the crime. The marked-up almanac showed premeditation. The staggered times of death showed a lack of remorse.

But the pièce de résistance was the retainer check that Shira Burr wrote out to Donna Nast on her private account. It was on that account that Nasty requisitioned banking statements and saw where else Shira's money went. Nasty traced the payoffs to cover Winston's affairs and the confidentiality agreements that Yasmine had discovered and used to blackmail her boss.

Means, motive, and opportunity.

Nasty had also noticed the blue rose petal on the floor of the locker room of the pool the morning we'd met. From there, she'd combed through bank statements, looking for payments to the florist, and discovered they'd ceased after Winston disappeared.

Before the case was solved, the press focused on Winston Burr. They'd dug around for clues in his background that tied him to old business partners, jilted lovers, and jealous husbands, but the reality was far simpler than that. Two wives who saw money as the solution to all their problems. Yasmine Garcia's blackmail plan pushed Shira to lengths she hadn't had to go when a simple six-figure payout was all it took to maintain the illusion that she and her husband had the perfect life.

Since good old-fashioned police and detective work exposed Shira for her crimes, my role as finder of a body in a trash can remained a detail in a police file. It was the kind of story the press would have loved. Naturally, I kept it to myself.

In an unfortunate turn of events, the courts ruled in Brandon's favor. Mad for Mod assets were seized as part of the settlement. My legal team had argued that the name Mad for Mod was too connected to me to be of value to Brandon, so I came out of the whole mess with that and my business license, and not much more.

A WEEK after the case was closed, the Kimball Insurance Group contacted me about the repairs to my storefront. The investigation had been completed, the preliminary estimates calculated, and the money was available to be paid. I could have said no and used the money somewhere else, but I was a creature of habit who liked the life I'd designed. I authorized the repairs and asked to be notified when they were done, and for the next week, I did some deep soul searching and wondered if it would have been so bad to leave it all behind.

At four forty-five the following Thursday, while Connie was poring over business school options at my kitchen table, the insurance company called. "You're all set," the representative said. "The repair team had to replace your front door, so you need to arrange to get your keys. I wouldn't wait too long."

"I'm free anytime," I said.

"Can you make it now? They're still on-site and probably won't be done until after six."

"Sure," I said.

The rain had finally stopped. I was dressed in a full-skirted white cotton dress with a wide, colorful belt and flowered Keds. I shielded my face with a straw hat with colorful silk flowers tucked into the band. I clipped on Rocky's leash, and the three of us left. Rocky sat on Connie's lap and hung his head out the window while I drove, and I marveled at the joy you could see on the face of a Shih Tzu puppy. It was like he knew something exciting was up ahead.

I parked on a side street, and the three of us walked to the corner and down the street. A small crew of workers was putting tools into the back of a truck that was parked by the curb in front. The main one, a burly gentleman in a grungy white T-shirt, jeans, and tan leather work belt that matched his boots, looked up at me.

"Are you Madison Night?" he asked me.

"How'd you know?"

"You match your store," he said. He smiled appreciatively at Connie, who wore a T-shirt that said Bad Kitty.

As I got closer, I noticed Bianca across the street. She smiled and waved, and I waved back. She stood in the parking lot as if watching me take possession of my keys was the highlight of her afternoon. The workers gradually stopped what they were doing and moved away from the door.

The burly man met me halfway and dropped a set of keys into my palm. "Glad you came by today. I don't want to be anywhere close when word gets out. The last thing I need is for my wife to hear about this."

"I don't understand," I said.

"OMG," Connie said. She stood outside my showroom with her hands on my newly installed window and her face pressed up against the glass. She turned to me. "Madison, hurry up. You need to see this."

I closed my hand around the keys and approached the showroom. Through the glass, I saw one thing. Flowers.

Thousands and thousands of flowers. Roses, and lilies, and lilacs, and hydrangeas, and carnations. Flowers in planters on the ground and in vases on the tables. Yellow, white, pink, orange, lilac, green, blue, red.

I turned to the workers. "Who did this?"

"You don't know?"

I knew.

I unlocked the front door and stepped inside. A narrow path led to my desk, where a vintage crystal vase with two dozen Gerbera daisies sat on top of a Thank You note. It was the order I'd placed with By George that I'd forgotten all about, that must have arrived while I was away. I opened the card and read, "Night —thanks for your help with the case." The note was signed by Tex. After his name was a postscript: "I'm ready when you are."

I stared at the card while Rocky sniffed the showroom for new scents. Connie came back to my office and dropped into the chair in front of my desk.

"I may not be fluent in the language of flowers yet, but I think these flowers say your relationship with Captain Allen is no longer in the closet."

Connie was right. I might have been unsure of the future, but for the first time in a long time, everything was coming up roses.

ABOUT THE AUTHOR

After two decades working for a top luxury retailer, Diane Vallere traded fashion accessories for accessories to murder. She is a national bestselling author and a past president of Sisters in Crime. She started her own detective agency at age ten and has maintained a passion for shoes, clues, and clothes ever since. Subscribe to the Weekly DiVa, to get girl talk, book talk, and life talk, at www.dianevallere.com/weekly-diva.

ALSO BY

<u>Samantha Kidd Mysteries</u>

Designer Dirty Laundry

Buyer, Beware

The Brim Reaper

Some Like It Haute

Grand Theft Retro

Pearls Gone Wild

Cement Stilettos

Panty Raid

Union Jacked

Slay Ride

Tough Luxe

<u>Madison Night Mad for Mod Mysteries</u>

"Midnight Ice" Novella

Pillow Stalk

That Touch of Ink

With Vics You Get Eggroll

The Decorator Who Knew Too Much

The Pajama Frame

Lover Come Hack

Apprehend Me No Flowers

<u>Sylvia Stryker Outer Space Mysteries</u>

Fly Me To The Moon

I'm Your Venus

Saturn Night Fever

Spiders from Mars

<u>Material Witness Mysteries</u>

Suede to Rest

Crushed Velvet

Silk Stalkings

<u>Costume Shop Mystery Series</u>

A Disguise to Die For

Masking for Trouble

Dressed to Confess

<u>Mermaid Mysteries</u>

Tails from the Deep

Murky Waters

Sleeping with the Fishes

<u>Nonfiction</u>

Bonbons for your Brain